SAMMY FERAL'S DIARIES of WEIRD

VAMPIRE ATTACK

Books by Eleanor Hawken

Sammy Feral's Diaries of Weird

Sammy Feral's Diaries of Weird:
Yeti Rescue

Sammy Feral's Diaries of Weird:
Hell Hound Curse

Sammy Feral's Diaries of Weird:
Dragon Gold

Want to find out more about Eleanor?
Visit www.eleanorhawken.wordpress.com for
news, events and more!

SAMMY FERAL'S DIARIES of WEIRD

VAMPIRE ATTACK

Eleanor Hawken

Quercus

ACKNOWLEDGEMENTS

Thank you to everyone who supported and encouraged me whilst
I was writing *Vampire Attack*. Thank you to my wonderful family,
my incredible husband and his wonderful family, and to my ever
patient agent, Victoria, my editor, Sarah, and to everyone else at
Quercus Children's Books. And thank YOU, my readers, for taking
the time to follow Sammy Feral on his crazy adventures.

First published in Great Britain in 2014 by
Quercus Editions Ltd
55 Baker Street
7th Floor, South Block
London
W1U 8EW

Text copyright © Eleanor Hawken 2014
Illustrations copyright © Keiron Ward for Artful Doodlers 2014

The moral right of Eleanor Hawken to be
identified as the author of this work has
been asserted in accordance with the Copyright,
Designs and Patents Act, 1988.

This book is a work of fiction. Names, characters, businesses,
organizations, places and events are either the product of
the author's imagination or are used fictitiously. Any
resemblance to actual persons, living or dead, events or
locales is entirely coincidental.

1 3 5 7 9 10 8 6 4 2

For Caroline and Pauline,
Nonna and Nanna – thank you
for the babysitting!

Friday 1st October

'We have to help!' I said, reading the message that had been sent to our Crypto Crisis Centre Facebook page.

'No, we don't,' replied Donny.

I'd come over after school and Red had shown me the message straight away. We were hanging out Backstage at my family's zoo – the part that's closed off to the public. If people knew the truth about what lies behind the gates, their jaws would drop open like those of a hungry hippo on a rampage. Not only do my friends Donny and Red live in the Backstage offices, but it's where they keep their pets. Not cuddly cats and drooling dogs. Oh no . . . I'm talking about a phoenix, a gut worm, a fire-breathing turtle and a truth trout!

It's also where Donny and Red manage their cryptozoology business.

Cryptozoology = the study of weird animals.

I help Donny and Red investigate all their most unusual cases. Werewolves, yetis, dragons and the Hell Hound are just a few of the crazy critters I've had to deal with: It's just one weird adventure after another in my wacky world. And it looked as though another one was about to start . . .

I read the Facebook message again to make sure it was as unbelievably weird as I'd first thought:

2

Dear Crypto Crisis Centre,

I am writing to you in desperation. I live in a village called Barren Heath. About a month ago a strange sickness swept through like a plague – a plague that affected only the children.

Overnight every child in the village grew pale and thin. They no longer played outside in the sunshine, but stayed in their bedrooms in the darkness. They stopped eating – not just their vegetables, but chocolate and pizza too! No doctor could work out what was wrong with them, and no cure could be found. It was as though the life had been sucked out of them . . .

And just when we could bear it no longer, we awoke one morning to find that every child in the village had vanished.

Boys, girls, babies and toddlers – there are none left. They disappeared in the night and no one has seen them since. We have searched far and wide, but there is no trace of the missing children. They have simply vanished into thin air.

The police can't help us.
No one can help us.
You are our last hope.

Yours faithfully,
A friend

'But every child in Barren Heath has just disappeared!' I said to Donny, pointing to the screen. 'We *have* to do something!'

'*No*, we don't!' Donny said again.

I'm used to Red being a moody mongoose, but not Donny. Donny's the main man, and weird is his middle name – he usually can't wait to get stuck into cases like this.

DONNY

* **Job:** Cryptozoologist (someone who studies animals that supposedly don't exist)

* **Lives:** In the Backstage offices at Feral Zoo (the zoo my family owns)

* **Looks like:** A grey-haired alley cat in a leather jacket

* **Talent:** He's a walking encyclopaedia of all things weird

RED

* **Job:** Cryptozoologist

* **Lives:** Backstage with Donny and all his weird pets

* **Looks like:** A miserable panda (she wears a TON of black eye make-up)

* **Talent:** The power of telekenesis (she can move things using only her mind – how cool is that?!)

ME

* **Job:** I earn my pocket money working at the zoo. I'm also a cryptozoologist in training!

* **Lives:** Tyler's Rest – a village where nothing happens unless you're me!

* **Looks like:** A tree frog with a freckly face

* **Talent:** I have the power of CSC – Cross-Species Communication (which means I can speak the languages of weird animals)

'Why don't you want to help?' I asked, confused.

'We deal with weird animals,' Donny replied, 'not cases of missing children. That's for the police to worry about, not us.'

'But the police can't find the children. The message said so . . . Maybe we should at least go to Barren Heath and see if—'

'I don't think there's anything we can do to help,' Donny said sternly, turning his back on me to feed his truth trout. The large fish shimmered blue as Donny dropped food pellets into its tank – meaning that Donny was telling the truth – he really didn't think we could help.

Bummer!

I turned to Red, hoping that maybe she'd back me up – she was the one who had shown me the message after all. But she simply shrugged her shoulders and gave a black-lipstick pout. 'Sorry, kid. Looks as if this is one weird adventure we won't be having.'

'Besides,' Donny added, moving away from the truth trout to feed his pet phoenix, 'it's October.'

'What does that have to do with anything?' I asked.

'What's at the end of this month?' Red asked, as if I was stupid.

The end of October = Halloween.

'Halloween,' I replied. 'But what . . . ?'

'Weird animal sightings always increase around Halloween,' Donny explained, refilling the phoenix's water bowl. 'Over the next few weeks we're going to get a lot of messages asking for help. Gremlin invasions, limping lindworms, genies escaping from their bottles, wailing banshees . . . Let's just hope we don't have to deal with a hissing hinkypink this year. It took me nearly a month to pull out the tooth that was left in my arm after one bit me last Halloween. I still have the scar, look!' Donny

pulled up his sleeve and
thrust his arm at me.

Wow, hissing
hinkypinks must
have mega-sharp
teeth. That scar
did not look
pretty!

'You'd better
prepare yourself
for a busy month,
Sammy,' Donny said,
pulling his sleeve down
again. 'I think it would be a good idea if you
started having proper cryptozoology lessons.
We can start tomorrow.'

'Proper lessons?' I raised an eyebrow.

Don't get me wrong – ever since I met
Donny there's nothing I've wanted more than
cryptozoology lessons. But sitting in a stuffy

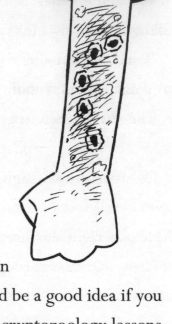

classroom isn't really Donny's style – so I've been learning on the job instead. 'Isn't it a bit late for that, Donny? I've been working with you and Red for ages. Stuff the lessons – let's go looking for hissing hinkypinks instead!'

'Trust me, you don't go looking for a hissing hinkypink,' Donny said. 'They come looking for you. And when they do, you need to be ready.'

The truth trout shimmered blue as Donny spoke.

He was right. He usually was.

There was no way I wanted a scar like the one on Donny's arm. Ouch! If a hissing hinkypink came looking for me, then I needed to know how to do battle with it. And with Halloween just around the corner, I didn't have long to prepare for whatever was coming my way.

But as I walked home from the zoo this evening, it wasn't Halloween that was playing on my mind. It was the message about the missing children. We couldn't just ignore it, could we? Maybe it didn't have anything to do with weird animals, but a whole village's worth of children doing a vanishing act registers a healthy 9 on the Feral Scale of Weirdness.

There must be something we can do?

I know Donny's right – we don't have experience in missing children; we have experience in werewolves (my family are all ex-werewolves!), yetis and dragons. But still, whoever messaged us wouldn't have bothered unless they thought we could help them.

Maybe weird animals have something to do with the missing children.

They could have been spirited away by sprites . . . or covered with panda snot and turned invisible . . . or eaten by trolls!

Children don't just vanish into thin air.

If I can find a link between weird animals

and the missing children of Barren Heath, then Donny and Red will have to help.

But what kind of crazy creatures can make children disappear?

Whatever the answer is, it can't be good . . .

Saturday 2nd October

'So, let's recap,' Donny said, pointing at the whiteboard. He'd turned one of the Backstage offices into a classroom and I'd spent the whole morning having my first formal cryptozoology lesson.

Yes, it's Saturday. Yes, I'm meant to be scrubbing the pygmy-hippo tanks. Yes, Mum will probably blast me into hyperspace with an ultrasonic scream when she finds out I've skipped out on my zoo chores. But I want to be a cryptozoologist one day, so crypto-classes come first.

I was secretly hoping I might learn about a

weird animal that I could link to the missing children. But so far there's been nothing. All Donny's wanted to teach me about this morning are hissing hinkypinks.

HISSING HINKYPINKS

Can be found: Living in sewers

Favourite food: Decomposing toilet paper

Look like: Bald pink rats with webbed feet and gills

Interesting fact: They are allergic to children and puke up radioactive sludge at the sight of them

Did you know: Hissing hinkypink vomit emits UV light. It lights up the sewers like daylight.

Donny tapped on the whiteboard. 'A hissing hinkypink can be found . . .'

'In a sewer,' I said quickly.

'And what do they eat?'

'Decomposing toilet paper.'

'Very good. And how can you fight one?'

'By spraying it with disinfectant.'

'And what else?'

I blinked at Donny.

'What else?' he repeated.

I shrugged. 'I can't remember.'

'Sammy, we've been through this twice this morning!'

'I know, I know.' I got up and started to pace around the room in frustration. 'I know it's important to learn this. I know there's more than one way to fight off a hissing hinkypink. But don't you think it's also important to find out what's happened to those missing children?'

'Not this again.' Donny sighed. 'I've already

told you, Sammy, the missing children are a matter for the police, not for us.'

'How can we say that for sure without investigating?'

'Sammy —' Donny sat on the edge of the table, pushed his grey hair out of his eyes and looked at me seriously — 'there's more to being a cryptozoologist than knowing how to fight off a hissing hinkypink. Sometimes we have to make tough decisions. We can't help everyone.'

I glanced at the truth trout, who was bobbing around happily in his tank. He glimmered a bright blue as Donny spoke.

How could Donny possibly be telling the truth?

How could it ever be a good thing to ignore someone who needed our help?

He's talking bananas!

'Well, if that's really what cryptozoologists

believe,' I said, staring Donny right in the eye, 'then maybe I don't want to be one.'

I didn't mean that. Cryptozoology pumps through my heart and flows through my veins. I love all animals, even weird dangerous ones. And I was born with a special talent for speaking the language of strange animals. I can speak Yeti, Dragon, Werewolf and Troll. There's nothing in the world I want to be more than a cryptozoologist.

But I was angry, and sometimes I say stupid things when I'm angry.

'Sammy, wait . . .' Donny called after me as I stormed out of the Backstage office, slamming the door behind me.

I stomped through the yard, ignoring Donny calling my name. I charged past Red, who was sitting on the ground bending spoons with the power of her mind. I didn't want to speak to her – she would only repeat what Donny had said.

I swept past the wish frog without even looking at him.

'Sammy! Sammy!' The wish frog hopped along after me.

WISH FROG

* **Looks like:** An Amazonian horned frog

* **Lives:** In hiding at Feral Zoo

* **Talent:** Can grant wishes (although technically he's retired)

* **Top-secret fact:** Wish Frog is the last of his kind. If he hopped into the wrong hands, it would be a DISASTER!

I stuck my nose in the air and charged on. I refused to believe that there was nothing we could do to help!

I don't care what Donny says. I would rather clean my teeth with porcupine bristles and turtle-poo toothpaste than give up!

'Sammy, wait!' The wish frog landed on my shoulder. 'Calm down. I need to speak to you.'

'If it's about giving up on those missing children, then I'm not listening,' I replied, trying to ignore him.

'Sammy, Donny's right . . .' The wish frog started to explain.

'Sammy Feral!' screamed Mum's voice from behind the monkey enclosure.

Busted!

Great – that's all I need, a blasting, Mum must have discovered that I haven't scrubbed out the pygmy-hippo tanks yet.

'Family meeting in Dad's office,' she boomed. 'Now!'

MY FAMILY – MUM, DAD, GRACE AND NATTY, AND CALIBAN THE DOG

✱ Are all ex-werewolves

✱ Have excessive ear hair, a love of raw meat and freaky sense of smell (left over from their werewolf days)

✱ Mum once made a cup of tea for a yeti – she STILL complains about the stench they left behind in our kitchen!

'We'll talk about this later,' I said to the wish frog, turning towards Dad's office. 'I don't care what you or Donny or Red think. I won't give up!'

I pushed open the door to Dad's office as the wish frog whispered in my ear, 'Knowing when to walk away is not giving up.'

'Sammy, I'm not sure your pet frog needs to come to this meeting,' said Dad, who was sitting behind his desk.

'Dad, this isn't just any pet frog, it's the wish—' My sister Grace jabbed me hard in the ribs. That's when I noticed that Dad's office was filled with people.

Mum and Dad were there, along with my sisters Grace and Natty and our family dog, Caliban, but so were all the other zookeepers. My family might live in the world of weird, but the other zookeepers don't know that the little guy on my shoulder could a) talk, and b) grant their wildest wishes.

Imagine what would happen if they knew. Epic chaos!

'What's going on?' I asked Dad. 'I thought this was a family meeting.'

'Everyone here at Feral Zoo is like a big family,' Dad said with a grin. He stood up behind his desk, straightened his tie and smiled. 'And I'm pleased to announce to the family that we have decided to enter the annual Zoo of the Year competition.'

A cheer erupted around the office.

Feral Zoo has won 'Zoo of the Year' three times. It's a pretty big deal, and winning it again would be AMAZING.

'Cool!' I smiled.

'We've got a good chance of winning the title again,' Mum said, standing beside Dad. 'But it's important that we work together as a team over the next few weeks to get the zoo into tip-top condition ready for the inspection.'

'Inspection?' Natty asked.

'There's always an inspection.' Grace rolled her eyes. 'The only reason you don't remember the inspection last year is because Mum wouldn't let you leave the house in case you ran around the zoo like a demented chipmunk!'

'I won't do that this year,' Natty said seriously. 'I'm six years old now.'

Dad cleared his throat and said, 'Feral Zoo will be inspected for cleanliness, research facilities, quality of animal enclosures, tastiness of the cakes in the zoo cafe – all the usual things.'

'What can we do to help?' asked Max. He's one of the zookeepers and also Grace's boyfriend (yuck!).

'I've drawn up a rota with everyone's name on it.' Mum began to hand out pieces of paper. 'Over the next few days and weeks everyone needs to take on extra zoo duties.'

'Even me?' I blurted out without thinking.

Mum gave me a look that could have frosted over a frothing volcano. 'Yes, Sammy, even you. You have extra cleaning duties.'

Extra cleaning duties = RUBBISH!

Trust Mum to ruin my plans.

How am I meant to help find the missing children if I have to spend every night of the week shovelling parrot poo? How is this fair in any universe?

After the family meeting I said goodbye to the wish frog and left the zoo in a serious grump. I walked home on my own, deep in thought.

First Donny and Red say that we can't help the missing children, and now Mum wants me to spend every spare minute of the day cleaning the zoo. How am I ever going to find the time to figure out what happened to those kids? Maybe I could do some research tonight . . . Maybe

I could fire up my computer and try to find a link between the children and weird animals . . . Maybe that way I can . . .

SKID!

HOP!

SPLAT!

I tripped over something black and furry and fell smack-bang flat on my bum.

Mega-ouch!

I got to my feet, rubbed my sore behind and looked down to see what had tripped me up.

It was a small black cat, looking up at me with piercing green eyes.

'Miaow,' the cat growled at me.

'Watch where you're going, cat!' I grumbled, shaking my head and walking away.

The black cat let out another sour miaow and ran ahead of me.

I crossed the road by the park, and the cat crossed too.

'Miaow, miaow,' it yowled at me. 'Miaow, miaow, miaow, miaow, miaow!' The cat became louder with every 'miaow', as if it was shouting at me. Weird.

I turned the corner by the sweet shop and the black cat was one step ahead of me. 'Miaow!' Is it possible for cats to be annoyed? Well, if it is, this cat was as ticked off as a tired terrapin. 'Miaow! Miaow! Miaow!' the creature bellowed, running along at my heels.

Most people might jump aboard the freak train if a black cat started shouting at them. But not me. Oh no! Cat wrath registers as a measly 2 on the Feral Scale of Weirdness.

'Miaow! Miaow! Miaow!'

The black cat ran between my legs and I nearly fell flat on my bum a second time.

'Hey!' I shouted down at the cat. 'Watch where you're going!'

Am I now a magnet for any daft old animal – not just the weird ones? What does it want? Milk . . . catnip . . . cuddles and snuggles? Don't look at me, cat! I've got weird animals and zoo animals to worry about. Run along and be someone else's pet kitty.

The cat let out a frustrated purr as it walked up my garden path and sat down on my doorstep. 'Miaow! Miaow! Miaow!'

'You're not having any milk off me,' I tutted. 'Shoo!'

The cat swished its tail about angrily and arched its back, hissing at me before running down the garden path and leaping up on to our garden wall, where it sat down and glared at me.

As I took my house keys out, something on the doorstep caught my eye.

It was an envelope with my name on it. The black cat had been sitting on top of it.

The Feral Scale of Weirdness was beginning to twitch . . .

I picked up the envelope with one hand and opened the front door with the other. Then I slammed the door behind me, drowning out the sound of the black cat that was still miaowing away in my front garden.

I ripped open the envelope and read the note inside.

It looked as though a two-year-old had picked up a pencil and written it . . .

THE CHILDREN OF
BARREN HEATH
NEED YOU . . .

Sunday 3rd October

1 A.M.

I haven't slept. I've been lying in bed, tossing and turning all night, thinking.

I'm as bamboozled as a barmy baboon.

After I'd read the note I looked up and down the street, trying to see if anyone was lurking in the shadows. Then I kept peeking out through the curtains, hoping to spy the mystery note-writer sneaking back in the dead of night. But there was no one. Whoever had left it was long gone. The only thing I could see was the black cat — it sat on the wall outside my house all evening, miaowing away.

I can't sleep. I need to speak to whoever wrote that note. I need to know what they mean — *The children of Barren Heath need you*. I want to help them, but how?

4 A.M.

I was finally drifting off to sleep, my eyes growing heavy and my breathing deeper, when a thought crash-landed in my brain like a free-falling fledgling.

The black cat!

Something about that furry feline wasn't quite right. In fact, it was distinctly weird . . .

I sprang out of bed and rushed down the stairs, out the front door and into the chilly night.

'Cat! Cat!' I called out.

But the black cat was nowhere to be seen.

I looked in the bushes, behind the rubbish bin and in the neighbours' gardens. Nothing. Not even a flick of a tail.

After sitting on our garden wall for hours, the black cat had vanished into the night.

Am I going mad from lack of sleep? Could a black cat really be the one trying to tell me something? Who knows . . . but right now I need to put my diary down and get some sleep. I'm exhausted!

7 A.M.

It was still dark outside as I revved up my computer and tapped 'Barren Heath Weird Animals' into the search engine . . .

Barren Heath is home to the county's fattest guinea pig . . .
Barren Heath hedgehog found hibernating in a car boot . . .
Barren Heath Labrador taught to dance the waltz . . .
Barren Heath's local bat population is on the rise . . .

There were loads of silly animal stories, but nothing that even hinted that weird animals were responsible for the missing children. And no mention of a black cat. Maybe I was just imagining that the cat was anything other than annoying.

As soon as it was light outside I headed downstairs and stuffed a handful of dry cereal and a few chocolate biscuits into my mouth for breakfast.

'Biscuits are not breakfast food!' Mum shouted from upstairs.

Seriously, how does she know what I'm doing when she can't see me? Not only do mums have eyes in the back of their heads, but in walls and kitchen cupboards too! 'And don't forget your extra cleaning duties at the zoo,' she called after me as I walked out the front door.

As if I could forget! Mum would probably rather I was scooping out skunk poo with my bare hands than trying to work out how a village of children could just vanish into thin air. To say she doesn't like me getting neck-deep in weird mysteries is the understatement of the century!

I was desperate to show Donny and Red the note that had been left on my doorstep. But not before I caught up on my zoo chores. I needed to get Mum off my case.

I spent the morning scrubbing out the sea lions, feeding the elephants and counting the newt spawn. After the last blob of newt spawn had been logged, measured and examined, I made my way Backstage.

I pushed open the office doors to find Donny with his head in a book and Red busy floating frozen field mice into the gut worm's tank using only the power of her mind.

'Donny, you need to see this,' I said, thrusting the note at him. 'It was waiting for me on my doorstep last night!'

'You wrote that, Sammy,' said Donny, looking up from the piece of paper and raising his eyebrows, 'with your toes!'

'No, I didn't,' I argued. 'Why would you think that?' I went over to the truth trout and said very clearly, 'I did not write this note. I think it may have been written by a cat.'

The truth trout shone a glistening blue. Donny closed the book in his lap and eyed me thoughtfully.

I quickly told him and Red about the black cat who had followed me home last night.

'Did the cat try to speak to you?' Red asked.

I shook my head. 'No, just plain old "miaows".'

Donny opened his book again and began to read, before muttering, 'Well, it wasn't the cat

33

who wrote the note then. If there was anything special about that cat, you would have been able to speak to it. Nothing's changed, Sammy. There aren't any weird animals involved, so this isn't a mystery we can help with. I'm sorry. Besides, we've had a report in of a hissing-hinkypink infestation. We need to investigate that.'

'Well, I'm going to work out what happened without your help! You worry about the hissing hinkypinks and I'll worry about—'

'You should be worried about hissing hinkypinks too, Sammy!' Red shouted at me. 'If you want to be a cryptozoologist, then worrying about weird animals will be your job! You do still want to be a cryptozoologist, don't you?'

'Er, is a polar bear white? Of course I do – but I also want to find out what happened—'

'Well, if you want to stick with us, kid, then

you need to learn to do what you're told,' Red said with a frown.

'Please, Donny,' I pleaded.

I was close to getting down on my hands and knees!

'No, Sammy,' Donny said, getting to his feet and making his way towards the coat rack. 'No weird animals . . . no problem of ours.' He reached for his black leather biker jacket and shrugged it on. 'Whoever wrote this note, whoever sent us that message, has got us all wrong. It's terrible that all those children disappeared, but it's not our problem. The hissing hinkypinks are our problem. Sammy . . .' he said gently, seeing how annoyed I was with him, 'I wanted to give you another cryptozoology lesson today, but I have to go hissing-hinkypink hunting instead. We'll pick up where we left off with our lessons tomorrow, after school, OK?'

I nodded at him and hung my head with a sigh.

There was nothing I could say to persuade him to help. Not unless I could find a link between the missing children and weird animals.

There has to be *something*. I just know in my heart that there's more to this story than we already know. I need to find out what it is . . . fast!

Monday 4th October

Dear Crypto Crisis Centre,

Have you no heart? Do you not care at all that dozens of innocent children have vanished into thin air? What if I told you your village was next? I bet you'd do something then!
　　I really, really, really need your help. Please reply to this message.

Yours,
A friend

Donny, Red, the wish frog and I stood staring at the computer screen. No one spoke. Red had called me away from cleaning out the spider tanks to show me the message.

I broke the silence. 'Why are you showing me

this? Does it mean you're finally going to help?'

Donny shook his head. 'No. But I need you to reply to the message.'

'Saying what?' I asked.

'Saying that, yes, we do have hearts, but they're there to pump blood around our bodies – not to be blackmailed into helping out with every unfortunate case that comes our way.'

Jeez! Donny may have a heart, but sometimes it's colder than a sparrow in a snowstorm!

'This is more than just an "unfortunate case",' I pointed out. 'And if you really don't want to help, then you could at least be the one to send the message.'

'We're going out,' Red said, pulling on her coat and zipping it up.

'Where?'

'Hunting hissing hinkypinks,' Donny replied. 'And we won't be back soon.' He slung a heavy-looking bag over his shoulder. 'Your cryptozoology lesson will have to be postponed, again.'

'Well, don't expect me to come with you,' I said, grumpily. 'While you go swimming in the sloppy sewers looking for hissing hinkypinks, I'm going to prove that weird animals made the children of Barren Heath vanish.'

'Er, you weren't invited to come with us,' Red smirked. 'And you need to finish cleaning out the spider tanks, or your mum might spontaneously combust.'

I sat down at the computer with a huff and folded my arms angrily. I didn't even wish Red and Donny luck as they waved goodbye.

'It's not fair,' I muttered to the wish frog when we were alone. 'I'm always being left out by those guys.'

'If you find a link between weird animals and the missing children, then they won't have a choice but to include you,' he said, before hopping after a passing fly.

The wish frog was right. If I wanted to be part of the action, then I needed to take matters into my own hands.

I hit 'Reply' on the computer.

 Dear friend,

Of course we have hearts! And our hearts do a lot more than just pump blood around our bodies. We are cryptozoologists and we devote our lives to helping others. There's no situation too dangerous, no animal too weird. But that's the thing . . . we investigate weird animals, not missing children.

Why did you contact us?

There must be a reason why you think cryptozoologists are better qualified to help solve your mystery than the police.

If there is any chance, no matter how small, that a weird animal may be involved in this case, then we can help. Could the children have been tricked away by trolls? Gobbled up by gremlins? Torn limb from limb by hissing hinkypinks?

Think carefully and get back to me . . .

Your friends,

Crypto Crisis Centre

I pressed 'Send' and sat back and waited for a reply to ping into the inbox. I waited and I waited and I waited . . .

Nothing.

It was growing dark outside and I had to be home in time for dinner.

And Red was right – if I slacked off finishing my chores, then there was a strong possibility that Mum would explode with anger.

And I didn't want Mum exploding.

Annoyed that I hadn't had an instant reply from the mysterious messenger, I left Backstage. After quickly cleaning out the rest of the spider tanks (a new batch of tarantulas had just hatched – so cute!) I headed home.

It was properly dark outside now and the moon was high in the sky.

Shivering from the cold, I walked faster and rubbed my hands together, trying to keep warm. I glanced up at the moon again and noticed something flying over it.

It was larger than a bird.

Smaller than a plane.

I recognized the shape instantly.

It was a bat.

A HUGE bat.

It looked larger than a golden-capped fruit bat, and they're the biggest bats in the world!

A second mega-bat soared through the sky, illuminated by the glowing moon.

I stopped walking and stared up, amazed. The sky was filling up with giant bats, hundreds of them. They swooped and soared through the sky, flapping their wings in unison and flying together like one mighty machine.

'Wow,' I mouthed in the darkness.

Bats are so cool.

But it was strange because we don't have a lot of bats here in Tyler's Rest. In fact, seeing any bats at all in my village is very rare.

I can feel the Feral Scale of Weirdness about to crank up a notch.

A swarm of giant bats in the sky is definitely weird, but what does it mean . . . ?

Tuesday 5th October

I stayed up late last night waiting for a reply to the message I had sent. But was there any sign?

No.

Nothing.

Big fat zilch.

I'm starting to wonder if this mystery 'friend' wants my help at all. Perhaps they've realized that there's nothing me or Donny or any other cryptozoologist can do to help.

Maybe it is time to walk away . . . Maybe there really is no connection between the missing children and weird animals.

I was so tired from staying up late that I slept right through my alarm clock. Instead I woke up to the sound of Mum bellowing up the stairs, 'SAMMY FERAL, IF YOU'RE NOT DOWN FOR BREAKFAST IN ONE MINUTE THEN I'M FEEDING IT TO THE DOG!!'

That woke me up!

I jumped out of bed like a joey on a trampoline. Boing!

No way do I want to brave school on an empty stomach.

I shoved on my uniform, which was still in a pile on the floor from last night. There was no time to dig out clean socks from my drawer so I did a quick sniff test on yesterday's. Hmmm, sweeter than dingo dung but not as stinky as a skunk. They would have to do.

'Er, Sammy, don't you wash any more?' My sister Grace pinched her nose dramatically as I sat down and poured myself some orange juice.

'No time for a shower this morning,' I replied, gulping down my juice. 'Or clean socks. I slept through my alarm. You might be able to smell day-old socks from the next room, but no one at school can. They'll never know.'

'NATTY FERAL, IF YOU'RE NOT DOWN FOR BREAKFAST IN ONE MINUTE THEN I'M FEEDING IT TO THE DOG!!'

I uncovered my ears as Mum finished yelling upstairs at my sister.

'Looks like you're not the only one who slept in this morning,' Grace said with a raised eyebrow.

Mum put a bacon sandwich in front of me and I chomped down on it like a starved wildebeest.

I was halfway through my second sandwich

when I heard the sound of
footsteps in the hallway.
Natty appeared at the
kitchen door in her
nightdress.

Mum did a double
take as she looked at my
little sister. 'Natty, why
aren't you dressed? You're
going to be late for school.'

'I'm not going to school,'
Natty whispered in a croak.

Mum went over to my little sister and put
a hand on her forehead. 'You're roasting hot!
And what's this strange bruise on your neck?'

Natty flinched away from Mum and quickly
slapped her hand over her neck.

'You'd better stay home today,' Mum said.
'Get back to bed and I'll bring you up some
breakfast.'

'Not fair!' I complained through a mouthful of bacon. 'How come Natty gets to stay off school and I—'

'Natty's sick, Sammy,' Mum snapped at me. 'Whereas you are perfectly healthy and you're going to go to school, and when that's finished you're going to go to the zoo and do her jobs as well as your own. For a start you can sweep out the otters until their enclosure shines like stars.'

I sat back in my chair in a sulk. I bet Natty's not really ill. I bet she's faking it. I mean, please – what kind of mystery illness starts with a weird neck bruise?

Before I left the house for school I had just enough time to check Facebook to see if I'd had a reply to my message.

Nothing.

I sighed as I turned off my computer and set off for school. As I walked along the road my feet squelched in something wet and sticky. I looked down — the pavement was covered in what looked like bird poo. Gross!

What kind of bird could poo that much? How could . . . ? Hang on a minute . . . this wasn't bird poo. Oh no! This was fresh-as-a-daisy, stinking, sloppy bat poo. Giant bat poo. A TON of bat poo!

I was so busy thinking about bat poo I didn't notice the black cat leap out in front of me.

'Miaow! Miaow! Miaow!'

My legs tangled with the furry critter, I lost my balance and fell flat on my face in poo — right outside the school gates!

The entire school saw—MEGA-embarrassing.

I got to my feet, brushing my trousers off and looking around for the black cat. Enough was enough – it had been following me around miaowing at me for days. What did it want?

My best friend Mark swaggered up to me with a cheeky chimp smile plastered on his face. 'Hey, Sammy, what is a black cat's favourite colour?' Mark is the king of bad jokes. 'Purrrrrple. Get it? Hahahaha!'

Ignoring Mark, I pushed my way through the crowd of schoolkids laughing at me, desperately looking for the cat.

But it was nowhere to be seen.

The school bell rang and I felt Mark tug on my arm, pulling me towards the classroom. 'Did you see that?' I asked him. 'I was tripped up by a black cat. I think there's something weird going on. I think the cat has been following me around and—'

'Quiet, please!' my teacher called as we entered the classroom.

I sat down behind my desk and opened up my school bag. There was an envelope with my name on it inside. It hadn't been there this morning.

W.H.A.T. is going on??

I quietly ripped open the envelope . . .

Sammy,
I thought you could speak to animals. Why do you keep ignoring me?
If you won't speak to me, then at least read this . . .
BEWARE OF THE BATS!

NO WAY!!!

My heart pounded in my chest!

I knew that cat was weird! It's been following me around for days, trying to speak to me. I don't speak Cat – I only speak the languages of weird animals. But what kind of non-weird animal can write letters?

The kind that can type emails?

The kind that might tell us about a village of missing children?

The kind that's warning us about bats?

All this time I've been looking for a link between the missing children and a weird animal, and now I have two – a weird cat AND a warning about bats.

This is too much! I felt as if my head was going to explode and splatter my frazzled brains all over the classroom walls!

I pulled out my phone and texted Donny

underneath my desk so the teacher wouldn't
see.

C U @ zoo 2nite. I have a weird animal
lead on the missing children

Donny texted back straight away.

C U 2morrow nite instead. Still out
hunting hissing hinkypinks.

How can this possibly wait until tomorrow?
How can I stop my head from exploding?!!

Wednesday 6th October

Good news – my head hasn't exploded yet. But Donny and Red STILL aren't back at the zoo. They're STILL away hunting hissing hinkypinks. I don't know when they'll be back. Donny won't pick up his phone when I call him. I'm desperate to talk to him about the bats and the black cat and the note it left in my school bag.

It's not like I've been able to speak to the cat about it either. Since tripping me up outside the school gates, it's done a disappearing act. I've been on the lookout for it at every corner I turn, but it's nowhere to be seen. I looked for it all last night and on the way to school this morning – no sign. I looked out of my classroom windows even more than usual – not a swish of a black tail in sight. I searched high and low, in bushes and under parked cars, on my way back home, but I found nothing.

A cat writing me a note warning me about bats and then vanishing into thin air = a solid 7 on the Feral Scale of Weirdness.

I stopped off at home on my way to the zoo, hoping the cat would try to trip me up as I walked up my garden path, but I was out of luck.

'Oh good, Sammy, you're home,' Mum said, looking flustered as I walked through the front door.

'Chill, Mum,' I said quickly. 'I know I need to go to the zoo to clean out the pot-bellied pigs. Everyone knows they poo more than a rhino with the runs! I'm on my way. I just stopped off to—'

'You're not allowed to go to the zoo this evening, Sammy,' Mum replied, looking at me over the top of her glasses. 'I want you to stay here.'

'Why? What about my chores?' I asked, confused.

'You'll have to do them over the weekend. Natty's still ill and I can't risk you getting ill too and spreading whatever's going around to the zoo visitors. You're quarantined until further notice.'

Quarantined?

How can I look for the black cat if I'm quarantined? I needed to go to the zoo! Donny might not be there, but I could speak to the wish frog about the note! 'But, Mum . . .' I began to argue.

'No buts, Sammy.' She wagged her finger at me. 'There's some kind of bug going around. All the children at Natty's school have it and I don't want you spreading it. Now do as you're told and take these up to your sister.' She handed me a plate of Natty's favourite dog biscuits. She prefers them to normal chocolate ones now that she's an ex-werewolf.

I shrugged my school bag and jacket off as I headed up the stairs with a frustrated sigh. 'I know you're only faking illness so you get out of shovelling pot-bellied-pig poo, Natty,' I said as I pushed open her bedroom door. I offered her the plate of pedigree pooch biscuits and expected her to wolf them down, but Natty just looked at them and turned up her nose.

'I'm sick,' she said feebly.

I stood back and took a long, hard look at my little sister.

To be fair, she looked terrible. Worse than a flea-infested ferret.

Her skin was pale, her cheeks were sunken

as if she hadn't eaten in a month and she was shivering even though she was wearing about ten layers of clothes. She even had a big fluffy scarf tied tightly around her neck.

'Natty,' I said, starting to feel concerned, 'you look as bad as Khan the tiger did that time he ate a tourist's backpack.'

Natty blinked at me and tilted her chin into the air, as if beckoning me to come closer to her. I shuffled forward. 'Sammy . . .' she whispered, with terror in her eyes.

I knew my little sister – something was wrong. Very, very wrong.

'Natty?' I whispered back.

'I need . . . I need . . .' she croaked, 'I need BLOOD!'

'I'll ask Mum to get some raw steaks in,' I reassured her. 'But you'll have to make do with these for now.' I put the plate of dog biscuits next to her bed and began to back away.

Wow. My sister's werewolf needs must be extra heightened because she's ill. She normally asks for raw meat, not blood! I really hope I don't catch whatever she has. I've got way too much to think about at the moment – I can't afford to be sick!

9 P.M.

I looked at myself long and hard in the mirror this evening. I don't feel sick. I don't have a temperature, a sore throat or tummy troubles. Fingers crossed, I have a super-strength immune system as well as the ability to talk to strange animals.

Thinking about all the extra zoo chores I would have to cover for Natty once I'm finally out of quarantine, I wandered over to my bedroom window to close my curtains for bed. As my hand reached for the material I stopped dead in my tracks.

My entire garden was covered in bats.

There must have been close to a thousand of them.

There were bats on the garden fence. Bats on the greenhouse roof. Bats hanging upside down from trees and plants and the washing line. Bats on the grass, on the flowerbeds, bobbing in the pond and hovering in the air above.

One bat hovered outside Natty's window. It was ginormous – bigger than any species of bat I'd ever seen. Its eyes shone red like magma and from its mouth protruded two giant fangs. Dripping from the fangs were long, slimy trails of drool. Gross!

Every one of them was facing my house, watching it.

BEWARE OF THE BATS. BEWARE OF THE BATS.

The message in the black cat's letter rang out in my head like an alarm bell.

The sight of hundreds of giant bats in the garden would register a healthy 6 on the Feral Scale of Weirdness at any time. But after the warning I'd had, the Scale of Weirdness was skyrocketing off the charts.

Beware of the bats.

What was I meant to do? Go out and fight them with my bare hands? Call the police? The fire brigade?

I did the only thing I could think of. I texted Donny . . .

Bat attack! Bat attack! Bat attack!

Thursday 7th October

I woke up this morning to a text.

Coming back 2 the zoo 2day. C U 2nite. D

Thankfully Mum's 'quarantine' didn't stop me from going to school. I knew she'd be mad at me for not coming straight home afterwards, but I had to go to the zoo. I had to speak to Donny. Now I had proof that weird animals had something to do with the missing children, it was time to get the investigation under way!

I ran through the zoo gates and headed straight for Backstage. I burst into the offices and flung my arms into the air when I saw Donny and Red sitting around the kitchen table.

'Giant bats are infesting the village. And a black cat *has* been writing me notes. The same cat who told us about the missing children. We have to –' I stopped speaking. A furry black face was looking in through the window.

'The black cat!' I screamed.

'What black cat?' Donny asked.

'That black cat!' I said, pointing at the creature perched on the kitchen windowsill. I marched over to open the window, and the cat leaped through.

'You've been ignoring me!' came a small voice from the kitchen floor.

I looked down in shock. The cat could talk? 'You speak English?'

A cat speaking English = 8 on the Feral Scale of Weirdness.

'Yes, but I thought you spoke Cat. I've been trying to talk to you for days!'

'I don't speak regular Cat. I only speak to weird animals—'

'Well, that explains why you've been so rudely ignoring me.' The black cat rolled its green eyes and spoke again. 'If I had known you didn't speak Cat, then we could have spoken days ago.'

'Whoa!' Donny got to his feet. 'What's going on? You left me a dozen messages, but not one said anything about a talking cat! I've never met a talking cat before,' he said with a glint in his eye.

'Not many people have,' the cat replied with a soft purr. 'We're very rare, and I'm the only talking female, as far as I know.'

'What's your name?' Donny asked.

'Sphinx,' the cat replied, sitting back on her hind legs and flicking out her tail.

'Why didn't you just speak English to me in the first place?' I asked Sphinx, confused.

'I was trying to be discreet,' she replied, lowering her voice to a whisper. 'What I have to say to you shouldn't be heard by just anyone.'

'And what's that?' Red asked.

'It's about the missing children of Barren Heath,' said Sphinx. 'That's if you care at all about helping them.'

'Of course we care . . .' Donny said, sitting back down and gesturing for Sphinx to join him. The cat leaped up on to an empty chair and then on to the table. She sat down opposite Donny and waited for him to finish talking. '. . . but we're cryptozoologists. We deal with weird animals. Not missing children.'

'Perhaps if you had signed your messages "Sphinx the talking cat", we might have been a bit quicker to reply!' I said.

'Like I said, I've been trying to speak to you for days,' Sphinx said, narrowing her green eyes.

'I have very sensitive information. I needed to know I could trust you.'

'So speak,' Red challenged her.

Sphinx eyed Red with distrust (and honestly, who could blame her? Red looks as friendly as a porcupine with a battleaxe).

'Barren Heath was once a lovely little town,' Sphinx said softly. The truth trout shone a beautiful blue in his tank. 'Full of green lawns and smiling children. Now it's a shadow of its former self.'

'Because the children went missing?' I asked.

'If you let me finish without interrupting, then I'll tell you,' Sphinx replied curtly.

Wow – talking cats are mega-moody!

I sat down and let Sphinx continue.

'It all started when the bats appeared. There were hundreds of them. They descended on the village like a plague. Everyone thought it was magical at first. Every night parents would take their children out to look at the bats. Some children gave them names, or tried to count them, even though there were far too many to keep track of.

'But then the children started to get sick . . .'

'What do you mean?' I asked.

'I'm getting there!' she snapped. 'They grew pale. They refused to go outside. In fact they shunned the sunlight completely – as if they were suddenly allergic to it. They stopped eating, and all they wanted to drink was blood. They craved it. The doctors didn't know what was wrong, and nothing the parents did seemed to help. Every day the children grew sicker, paler, thinner – as if they were fading away before their parents' eyes. As if the life was being sucked out of them . . .'

'Go on . . .' I said, dread rising up inside me.

'And then one day they were gone,' Sphinx said in a whisper. 'Vanished from their beds in the night. Not one child was left in the morning. That was the day the bats left too . . .'

'And you knew our village was in danger next?' I asked.

Sphinx nodded. 'They've come here, haven't they?'

I nodded back.

'Hang on a minute,' Donny said. 'Let me get this straight . . . In the last few days since we've been away you've seen a dramatic peak in the local bat population?'

'Yes,' I replied quickly. 'That's why I texted you "Bat attack!" Remember?'

'Well,' Donny said with a sigh, 'it would seem that we owe you an apology, Sammy. You were right all along. We can and we must help find the missing children. I'm sorry.'

I straightened my back and tried not to smile. Donny was hardly ever wrong, and it felt good to have been right all along. But being right wasn't the most important thing on my mind . . . 'Thanks, but there's something else you need to know.' I gulped. 'It's Natty . . . and all the other young children in Tyler's Rest . . . they're sick. Really sick. Just like you described, Sphinx.'

Sphinx arched her back and let out a small growl. 'The children of this town are in terrible, terrible danger. If we don't act soon, it will be too late.'

Friday 8th October

The situation is worse than a whistling walrus.

Sphinx is right — whatever the giant bats did to the children of Barren Heath to make them disappear, they're at it again . . .

'Is Natty feeling any better?' I asked Mum as soon as I got home from school.

Mum shook her head, looking worried. 'No. She hasn't left her room all day, and she won't let me open her curtains to let the light in. She's not eating — she keeps asking me to bring her blood to drink. I think she's delirious. Promise me you won't go in there,

Sammy. Whatever bug she's got, I don't want you picking it up too.'

Afraid of sunlight? Craving blood? This is exactly what happened to the children of Barren Heath before they disappeared. Sure, Natty can be as annoying as a squealing squirrel, but I don't want her disappearing into the night with a plague of bats.

I picked up my phone to text Donny – we needed to find a way to stop things getting any worse. But my phone beeped with a message from him before I had a chance to type . . .

Come 2 zoo 1st thing 2morrow. We're
going 2 Barren Heath 2 investigate!

Finally!

If we can find out exactly what happened to
the children of Barren Heath, then we might
be able to stop whatever happened there from
happening here too.

And who knows – maybe it's not too late
for the children of Barren Heath. Whatever the
bats have done with them, maybe there's still a
chance they can be saved . . .

Saturday 9th October

My brain is totally fuzzled from lack of sleep.

What kept me up all night?

Bats.

Giant, furry, fang-tastic, drooling bats.

I've been going round in circles wondering how bats can make children disappear, and this is all I've come up with:

* Pick the children up and carry them away into the night
* Eat them
* Scare them so badly they run away and never come back.

It makes no sense at all.

Sphinx was sitting outside the zoo gates when I arrived this morning. 'Good morning, Sammy,' she purred up at me. 'You know, a saucer of milk wouldn't hurt . . .'

'No time,' I replied, swinging the gate open and marching into the zoo. Sphinx ran along beside me. I charged past the giraffes, elephants and wildebeests without stopping. 'I need to go Backstage pronto. Donny's driving us to Barren Heath to investigate.'

I hurried through the Backstage gates, across the yard and swung open the office door. Donny and Red were busy feeding their pets. 'There has to be some kind of clue in Barren Heath,' I said to Sphinx, 'about how the bats made the children disappear.'

Sphinx sat down by the truth trout's tank and let out an unhappy purr. Her green eyes had clouded over and her whiskers were twitching nervously. I've lived in the world of weird long enough to know when I smell something fishy . . . and right now Sphinx smelt worse than a swordfish on a sunny day. 'What's wrong?' I asked.

'Nothing's wrong,' she said quickly.

The truth trout shimmered a violent red.

'You're lying,' Red said to Sphinx, putting down the bag of gut-worm feed and walking towards her.

Sphinx's tail began to swish from side to side. 'I'm not lying,' she said, sounding flustered. 'I'm fine. Absolutely fine.' The truth trout shone in shades of red. Sphinx was definitely not fine.

'You know, don't you?' I asked Sphinx. 'You know how the bats make children disappear. We don't need to go to Barren Heath to find out – you could save us the journey and just tell us now.'

The truth trout suddenly shone bright blue.

'We don't have time for this,' Donny said. 'I don't need Sphinx to tell us what we're dealing with. I already know.'

Rewind! Excuse me? What?

'You know how the bats make children disappear?' I asked, gobsmacked.

He nodded. 'I have my suspicions. But we need to visit Barren Heath anyway. You know my motto when it comes to weird animals . . .'

'Research, research, research,' I answered quickly. 'What are your suspicions?'

'I can't be sure –' Donny scratched his head – 'but giant bats, sick kids and blood cravings . . . you do the maths, Sammy.'

Er . . . Giant bats + sick kids + blood cravings = ???

I looked towards Sphinx for an answer.

'I'm coming with you,' Sphinx announced, springing to her feet. No answer there then.

'You're hiding something from us,' I said to

Sphinx as we all climbed into Donny's van.

Donny revved up the engine and drove us out of the zoo.

'I'm not hiding anything,' Sphinx said, turning her face away from me so I couldn't read her furry expression. 'I've told you everything I know.' She purred angrily.

We drove the rest of the way in frosty silence. It took a couple of hours to get to Barren Heath. Donny parked the van and we all trudged out into the cold street. The village was eerily quiet. The sky was a dark, threatening grey, the trees looked barer than any we'd passed on the journey and even the houses looked as though the life had been sucked out of them – as if the bricks were crumbling with rot and mould.

'So this is what a village with no children looks like.' Red shivered as she spoke.

Sphinx trotted on in front of us. 'Follow me. There's something you need to see . . .'

We followed the cat to an empty children's playground. The swings squeaked on their hinges. The roundabout creaked in the wind. Leaves rustled under the rusting slide.

The wind whistled in my ears, and I felt the cold creep into my bones as I looked around at the abandoned playground. It was like a wasteland.

A village without children = a horrible place to be. All I wanted to do was leave.

From the looks on their faces, Donny and Red felt exactly the same way.

'It's just as I suspected . . .' Donny started

to say, but he was cut off by the loud shouts of a woman from the other side of the park.

'You! You! You!' the woman shouted, running towards us. Her hair stuck up all over the place and she was wearing what looked like a torn nightdress and tatty slippers. She looked crazy!

'You!' she pointed at me. 'Matthew!'

'Um, sorry, lady,' I said. 'I'm not Matthew.'

'Matthew!' she cried, lunging towards me and grabbing me around the shoulders. She pulled me into her bony chest and wrapped her thin arms around me, squeezing me tight. 'My Matthew, you've come back.'

I tried to pull away, but the woman was freakishly strong. 'I'm not Matthew!' I shouted, trying and failing to push her off.

The woman began to drag me away, but I felt another set of hands come around me and drag me in the other direction.

'I'm sorry, madam,' Donny said firmly. 'There's been a mistake. This isn't Matthew.'

'Matthew, my boy!' the woman shouted louder, hugging me closer to her. She smelt of stale cabbage and unwashed hair. 'You've come back to me.'

Donny yanked the woman's arms away

from me and pulled me backwards. 'This isn't Matthew,' he said sharply.

The woman looked at me and her eyes filled with tears. 'My son, Matthew – he vanished one day and he hasn't come back.'

'I know,' I said as gently as I could. 'We want to help you find him. We want to find all the children who went missing.'

'Please,' she sobbed loudly. 'Bring my Matthew home to me.'

Donny looked the woman in the eye. 'What can you tell me about Matthew's disappearance?' he asked. 'Did you notice anything strange about him before he vanished? Anything out of the ordinary?'

The woman shook her head, tears streaming down her dirty face. 'He hadn't been well for weeks. So pale and tired. He wasn't eating, wasn't sleeping. Wouldn't go outside to play with his friends. But they were all ill too. They had these horrible, horrible bruises on their necks. The bruises got larger, darker every day. And then one day I went into Matthew's room in the morning and he had gone. The window was wide open, his bed unmade. It was as if he had simply got up and left in the middle of the night. I searched the garden, the park, the shops, his school and everywhere else I could think of. I couldn't find him. My Matthew has just gone. Vanished.'

'Is there anything else you can think of?' Red asked. 'Anything that seemed strange?'

'The only other thing . . .' She shook her head with a sob. 'But it's so silly, I don't know . . .'

'Nothing's too silly to mention,' I said quickly.

'It was the bats,' she whispered. 'There were hundreds of them here in the village when Matthew was ill. The only time he seemed happy in those last few weeks was when he was looking out of his bedroom window at night, as the sky filled up with bats. The local news said it was a freak migration. Thousands of bats coming to Barren Heath to make their home for the winter. But the day the children vanished, so did the bats. It was as if he had flown away with them, into the night . . .'

'We're going to do everything we can to find Matthew and bring him home to you,' Donny said to the woman. 'I promise.'

He wrapped his coat around the mother's shoulders and he and Red walked her back to her house, leaving me and Sphinx to go back to the van alone.

My mind went into overdrive – Matthew's mother's words repeated themselves over and over inside my head: *It was as if he had flown away with them . . . into the night.*

'The bats didn't just make the children

disappear, did they?' I asked Sphinx as we arrived at the parked van. 'They took the children with them, off into the night.'

Sphinx stayed silent, her green eyes staring off into the distance.

'The truth is more terrible than you could ever imagine, Sammy Feral,' she whispered eventually.

'Tell me one thing,' I said. She stared at me, her emerald eyes giving nothing away as she gave me the slightest nod. 'Is there something here, in Barren Heath, that we're missing?'

'There's nothing here for you,' she shook head. 'No piece to the puzzle. No fact or clue. Nothing. This place is as empty of information as it is of children.'

'Why did you let us come here?' I asked angrily. 'We've wasted time when we could have been doing research!'

'It's not a waste of time,' she replied. 'You

needed to see for yourselves how terrible a town without children truly is. Now you've seen it, you won't ever let it happen again.'

Sphinx was right. I'd rather wrestle a thousand cranky crocodiles than let another town suffer the same fate as Barren Heath.

Donny and Red arrived back at the van.

'Time to get out of this ghost town,' Red said sharply, opening the van door. 'I don't think there's anything here that will help us get to the bottom of what happened to those children.'

'There isn't,' I confirmed.

We all clambered in and began the long journey back to the zoo. For a while we drove in silence, each one of us lost deep in thought.

Mega-bats with dagger-sharp fangs, victims who crave blood and become afraid of sunlight. No way . . . it can't be possible . . . Of all the weird things I have seen . . .

I started to speak my thoughts out loud, 'Giant bats . . . sick children . . . blood cravings . . . If I didn't know better I'd think that . . .'

'Say it,' Red challenged me. 'We're all thinking the same thing.'

'But it can't be,' I whispered with dread. 'Do they even exist?'

Donny nodded.

Sphinx was right. The truth really was more terrible than I could have ever imagined.

Slowly I said the words out loud.

'Vampire bats.'

Sphinx gave the tiniest nod of her head. It was true.

Vampire bats had taken the children of Barren Heath, and if we didn't do something soon they'd take Natty and all the other kids in my village too.

Sunday 10th October

Vampire bats.

Bloodsucking, fang-tastic, coffin-creeping vampire bats. Big ones.

Vampire bats = a maxed-out 10 on the Feral Scale of Weirdness.

I barely slept a wink, haunted by the memory of the woman who mistook me for her son. I can't imagine how upset my parents would be if my sisters and I went missing. Plus I'd hate to never see my parents again. Mum might drone on about homework and zoo chores, and Dad might fart when he thinks no one's listening . . . but they're my parents, and I love them.

The sooner we find a way to rid the world of bitey-faced bats, the better.

So first thing this morning I rubbed my tired eyes and gobbled down a slice of toast with jam as I was heading for the front door. Just as I was about to sneak out of the house Mum came down the stairs. 'I hope you're heading straight to the Rare Animal Breeding Centre to sweep out the pandas, Sammy,' she said sternly.

'I'm not quarantined any more?' I asked hopefully.

Mum let out a loud sigh. 'I need you to help out at the zoo. The Zoo of the Year inspection is looming, and the pandas' enclosure is in need of a good sweep. But the *minute* you start feeling ill, I want you home. Understand?'

I nodded and threw my arms around her and squeezed her tight. 'I love you, Mum,' I said, pressing my face into her jumper.

'What's got into you, Sammy?' she said with

a frown as I pulled away from her. She pressed the back of her hand to my forehead. 'I hope you're not coming down with whatever Natty's got. I could always ask Max to sweep out the pandas.'

I shook my head. 'I just want you to know that if anything ever happens to me – or to any of us – that we love you and we really appreciate everything you do for—'

'Hang on a minute!' Mum said, sounding cross. 'You better not be getting mixed up in another one of Donny and Red's dangerous adventures again. Because if you are . . .'

'Bye, Mum!' I shouted over my shoulder, making a fast exit. I might be coming over all soppy from lack of sleep, but no way did I want to give my mum a reason to keep me away from the zoo!

As soon as I got to the zoo I headed straight to the panda enclosure. Not only did I have to keep Mum happy by cleaning them out, but the pandas can be pretty useful when it comes to all things weird. Most people think that pandas are just bamboo-munching bears, but they're wrong.

Pandas are anything but normal. And Su and Cheng were even stranger still – they arrived at Feral Zoo with a dragon egg stashed away in their crate! But that's another story . . .

SU AND CHENG

* **Species:** Giant panda
* **Originally from:** China
* **Top-secret fact:** All pandas are as weird as a wonky winklefish!
* **Amazing ability:** Panda snot can turn things invisible

If I wanted to find a way to defeat a plague of vampire bats, then asking Su and Cheng for help was a pretty good place to start. It took me ages to find them in the panda enclosure. They'd hidden themselves underneath a giant pile of bamboo leaves.

'*What are you doing under here?*' I asked in fluent Panda, pulling the leaves off them. As with all weird animals with amazing abilities, I can speak to Su and Cheng.

'*Hey!*' Su growled at me. '*Quit messing with our camouflage — we're in hiding.*'

'*Why?*' I asked.

'*Cheng woke up this morning with a little . . . blemish,*' Su pointed out.

It wasn't little. Cheng had a pus-filled spot the size of a golf ball on her nose!

'She doesn't want the zoo visitors to see her when she's not looking her best.'

A proud panda with a pimple = a healthy 4 on the Feral Scale of Weirdness.

'Whatever.' I shook my head. 'I promise to cover you both up again as soon as you answer a couple of questions I have.'

'Questions about what?' Cheng sighed as she scratched at the spot with her paw. 'How to turn yourself invisible with panda snot? How to catch a troll? How to tame a dragon?'

'No. I know all that stuff. I need you to tell me everything you know about vampire bats.'

'Vampire bats?' Su said thoughtfully, chewing on a stick of bamboo. 'Why would you want to get mixed up with them?'

I quickly told the pandas everything that had happened. I told them about the children of Barren Heath going missing, and Natty being sick.

'What do we need to do to get rid of them?' I asked. 'Have you ever heard of something like this happening before?'

'We're pandas, not walking encyclopedias,' Su replied with a yawn.

'Yes, but you are very wise creatures who know something about everything,' I pointed out, hoping flattery would get me what I needed – information!

Cheng smiled smugly. 'You're right, we do know a little about everything – even vampire bats.'

Bingo!

'Do you remember, Su, that time in Chengdu when a whole village of children disappeared?'

'Yes, I do remember that – it happened at the same time as a sharp peak in the local bat population.'

'If I remember correctly,' Cheng continued, 'the bats appeared one night and no one knew why . . .'

'The village had never been home to a bat colony before. But before anyone could establish why, the bats had disappeared into the night as quickly as they had arrived. Only it wasn't just the bats that disappeared. The village's children disappeared too.'

'Did they ever come back?' I asked impatiently.

'Actually they did,' Su replied. My ears twitched in delight at his words. 'Years later, *after their parents had grown old and grey, the children all came back.'* Years later? The smile began to slip from my face: this did not sound good. *'The strange thing was, they hadn't aged a day. They had been missing for years and yet they looked exactly the same as the day they had vanished. The only thing different was that they were not alone. They came back to their village with a stray cat. Do you remember, Cheng?'* Su asked his mate. *'The black cat stayed in the village until those children had grown old and had children of their own. Such a strange story . . .'*

There is no such thing as coincidence. Not when it comes to weirdness.

I'd bet a year's supply of bamboo that the black cat in Su's story was the same black cat who came to warn us about the bats – Sphinx!

I lunged forward and flung my arms around Su's neck. I gave him a huge kiss on his fuzzy cheek. *'Thank you!'*

'*Now cover us back up before the zoo visitors spot us and want to point and stare at Cheng's unfortunate pimple,*' he said, pushing me away.

I covered Su and Cheng back up with bamboo leaves, quickly finished cleaning out their enclosure and headed for Backstage. The pandas' story had given me proof that Sphinx knew more than she was letting on – and now it was time for her to spill the beans!

But when I got Backstage the place was as empty as a hungry hippo's tummy. There was no sign of Sphinx, Donny or Red.

'They had to investigate another hissing-hinkypink sighting,' said a small voice from the bookshelf. 'Strange animal sightings really do increase this time of year, you know.'

'Hi, Wish Frog,' I said. 'Never mind hissing hinkypinks, it's Sphinx I'm after. It's time for that talking fuzzball to cough up the truth!'

'Never trust a talking cat, that's what I

always say,' the wish frog said wisely. He leaped off the bookshelf and on to my shoulder. 'I take it this is about the bats?' I nodded. 'Have you seen this book here?' He pointed to a leather-bound volume on the top shelf. 'I think you might find it an interesting read.'

I pulled out the book the wish frog was pointing to and looked at the front:

It wasn't a talking cat. But it was better than nothing.

I spent the rest of the day helping out around the zoo. I fed the lions, shovelled elephant poo, strung up hay bales for the zebras and counted the new tadpoles that had hatched in the amphibian house (342!).

After dinner I went to my room and opened up *The Behaviour of Bats*. The first few chapters were pretty standard. Everyone knows that bats have super-powered hearing and that they use ultrasonic pulses to hunt.

But by the fifth chapter, things had got interesting . . .

CHAPTER FIVE
VAMPIRE BATS

THERE ARE FOUR known sub-species of Vampire Bat: the Common Vampire Bat, the Hairy-Legged Vampire Bat, the White-Winged Vampire Bat and the lesser-known Weird Vampire Bat.

The first three sub-species can be found in South America, and are often studied in zoos. However, the Weird Vampire Bat is considered a mythical creature – most people do not believe it exists.

But Weird Vampire Bats do exist. And they are incredibly dangerous. Weird Vampire Bats roam from village to village, feeding as they travel and never returning to the same place twice. They like to feed on defenceless creatures, most commonly children and small animals. Their bite is incredibly contagious and once bitten a victim will . . .

A strange noise outside my room made me look up. I opened my bedroom door and the noise grew louder.

It sounded like sucking . . .

And it was coming from Natty's room.

'Natty?' I called out.

There was no answer.

'Natty?' I said again, as I walked towards my little sister's bedroom door.

Slowly I reached for her door handle, turned it and pushed. The sound of sucking filled my ears as I stood in the doorway, paralysed with terror at what I saw.

The window was wide open and there were hundreds of bats flying around inside Natty's room. There were bats hanging upside down from the bookshelves, the lampshade and even all over the papier-mâché hamster Natty had made for her school art project. But most terrifying of all was the sight of dozens of bats swarming around my little sister's body as she slept soundly in her bed. Trails of bat drool dripped on the carpet, soaking everything it fell upon.

One giant mega-bat – bigger than all the other bats I'd seen – rose higher into the air and looked down at my sister, who seemed so small and frail among the swarm of flapping, drooling bats.

'Natty Feral,' the giant bat snarled, 'we've come back for you, just like we said we would. Are you ready for us?'

I couldn't hear my sister's reply.

All I heard was the shriek of excited bats as they swarmed in closer.

'Natty!' I screamed.

The chief bat swung around at the sound of my voice. He had blood dripping from his fangs – Natty's blood! 'It's too late for your sister.' The bat spat flecks of blood as it hissed. 'She's ours now. *We'll be back, and next time we're coming for you . . .'*

The giant bat beat his wings together and rose into the air. He must have emitted some kind of ultrasonic noise that I couldn't hear, but the other bats could. All at once they pulled away from my sister and swarmed out of her bedroom window.

Natty's curtains flapped in the cold breeze as the sound of the bats flying off into the night faded away.

My shaking legs carried me over to Natty's bed and I looked down at my little sister.

She was covered in tiny fang marks. But as I watched, they started to disappear, as if by magic. And the only mark left on her body – the only sign that something had attacked her – was a small bruise on the side of her neck.

Monday 11th October

'You saw the bats attacking Natty?' Donny repeated down the phone.

'YES!' I shouted. 'I've been trying to get hold of you all night. Never mind the hissing hinkypinks – this is way more important.'

'I agree, Sammy, vampire bats are a problem,' Donny agreed, 'but so are hissing hinkypinks. We haven't got our hands on one yet, but we know they're there – the sewers are splattered with their UV vomit.'

Er, rewind: vampire bats . . . a problem?

Leaping lemurs! Toothache is a problem. B.O. is a problem. A winking wart on the end of your nose is a problem. Vampire bats are a deadly catastrophe!

'But that's not all,' I said, feeling flustered. 'I spoke to the pandas yesterday and they told me that this has happened before. And there's a cure – there must be, because when it happened before the missing children came back. It was years later – that part of the story wasn't great news. But the point is that they did eventually come back. And Sphinx was with them. We need to find that critter of a cat – she needs to cough up every hairball of truth she's hiding from us.'

'OK, we'll be at the zoo tonight,' Donny replied. 'Yesterday's hissing-hinkypink report was a false alarm anyway. Just regular old flying pixies. See you later, Sammy.'

The one good thing I have to go on is the fact that Natty hasn't sprouted wings and flown away into the night yet. Whatever the vampire bats do to children to make them vanish, they haven't done it here yet. I checked on her this morning and she was asleep in her bed. Pale as a puking pufferfish, but still there. Maybe the giant bat who spoke to me was wrong; maybe it isn't too late for Natty.

One thing's for certain – those bloodsucking beasts are not getting within an inch of my sister again. There's no way I'm watching the all-you-can-eat Natty Feral Bat Buffet take two!

And as for Sphinx – that cat's days are well and truly numbered. I don't know what game Sphinx is playing, but I am about to tear up the rule book and set the pitch alight!

I'm going to get the truth out of her if it's the last thing I do!

But first, I needed to go to school. (It was Monday, after all . . .)

'What do you mean, you haven't done your history homework?' Mrs Nelson shouted at Tommy Smith this afternoon.

Yep, that's right — Tommy was getting a blasting today, not me!

'Sorry, Mrs Nelson,' Tommy replied. 'My little brother's been really ill and I've had to help look after him. No one knows what's wrong. The doctor says it's the same thing all the other young kids in the village have. He's got a high temperature, he hates sunlight, he won't eat his food and he's got this really weird bruise on the side of his neck.'

Alarm bells started to ring inside my head.

Bruise on neck = bad news!

'That sounds like the same thing my little sister has,' said Katrina to Tommy.

'My brother's ill at the moment too,' said Freddie.

'And my brother!' said Simon.

That confirms it. The town is under vampire-bat attack. If I don't find a way to help, then very soon Natty and the rest of her school will be sprouting fangs and flying away into the night.

I grabbed Tommy's arm as soon as history was over. 'Sorry to hear about your brother,' I said quickly. 'I don't suppose you've noticed anything strange around your house lately?'

'Like what?' Tommy looked confused.

'Like large bats in your garden at night?'

Tommy's eyes lit up. 'Now you mention it, yes. Our garden's been full of bats the last few nights. They've been hanging from the trees and pooing all over my dad's shed. But what does that have to do . . . ?'

I didn't stop to hear the rest. I needed to get to the zoo – fast!

I charged into the Backstage offices like a shark speeding towards prey.

'It's time to find Sphinx,' I said to Donny, without even bothering to say hello.

'I'm right here,' Sphinx said with a purr,

looking up from a saucer on the floor and licking cream off her lips.

I looked around in astonishment. Donny was calmly writing in his notebook, Red was tapping away on her computer and the wish frog was perched on Red's shoulder, looking at her computer screen. 'Er, excuse me!' I shouted at everyone. 'There's a traitor in our midst –' I pointed at Sphinx – 'and everyone is acting as cool as cucumber.'

'We've been waiting for you to arrive, Sammy,' Donny flipped his notebook shut.

'There's something I need to tell you,' Sphinx said in a low growl. 'I wanted everyone to be here when I said it.'

'You're working for the bats!' I pointed an angry finger at the black cat. 'You knew all along that it was weird vampire bats we were dealing with! You knew they were coming here to attack the children. You're on their side – it's the only possible explanation. You're trying to buy them time so they can suck the life out of every child in this village before we can stop them. That's why it took days for you to speak to me. That's why you acted so strangely about our visit to Barren Heath. And that's why, when vampire bats attacked a village of children before, you were at the scene of the crime!'

'If I was working for the bats, would I really be trying to help you?' Sphinx hissed back.

I stomped towards her, anger boiling up inside me. Natty was having the life sucked out of her every night and we could have stopped it if we had known. 'Help us?! Now you listen to me, you sour, milk-swilling, lying little paw-licker . . . My sister and every other little kid in the village are becoming bat food! You know a way to stop them—'

'No, I don't!' Sphinx leaped in front of the truth trout's tank and the fish began to flicker in blue. My heart ground to a painful halt. The truth trout had to be wrong – Sphinx knew a way to stop the bats, surely!

'I am helping you. I told you to beware of the bats.' Sphinx angrily flicked her black tail. 'Trust me, Sammy Feral, you and I want the same thing.'

'And what's that?' I narrowed my eyes, trying my hardest not to shout.

'To stop the vampire bats from claiming any more victims.'

'So I suppose we should start researching weird vampire bats then.' Red shrugged.

'Sammy, you look at the books in Donny's library, I'll—'

'Not so fast,' I cut in. 'I bet Sphinx knows a lot more about weird vampire bats than we can read about in any book.'

Sphinx nodded and in one smooth movement leaped from the floor on to the kitchen table.

'Tell us,' I demanded. 'Tell us everything you know. And stay right where you are –' I pointed to the truth trout's tank – 'so we know if you're telling the truth.'

Sphinx sighed. 'Very well. I promise you I will tell you everything I know.' The truth trout glimmered in shades of peacock blue. 'But I want you to promise me something first . . .'

'Anything,' I said quickly, answering for everyone. If it meant getting the truth from Sphinx and being able to help Natty, then I'd do anything.

'Don't judge me. Whatever I tell you, no matter how bad it is, promise that you won't try to chase me out of Feral Zoo with a shovel.'

'We promise,' Donny, Red, the wish frog and I said at once.

Sphinx took a deep breath, and there was a moment of blistering silence before she spoke.

'I was once a normal house cat. I lived with a normal family, in a normal village. I ate normal food. I could only speak Cat and I did normal—'

'We get it,' I said impatiently. 'You were very normal.'

'But one day,' Sphinx continued, 'a plague of giant bats descended on our village. I was in our garden when they first attacked. They sank their teeth into my neck and I felt the life draining out of me. They visited me again the next night, and the next and the next. I don't remember when the change happened, but when it did I took to the skies and flew away with them.'

'You were a vampire bat?' Red blurted out, unable to hide the shock on her face.

Sphinx nodded.

Wow – I did NOT see that coming!

'I spent many, many years in a vast colony of vampire bats. Every colony is led by a chief bat – and our leader went by the name Zoomanna. Zoomanna led us from town to town, and everywhere we went we inflicted great pain and torture. I lost count of the number of lives I destroyed. I was truly, truly evil.'

'Why didn't you tell us this before?' Donny asked curiously.

'I wanted you to trust me before I told you

the truth.' Sphinx hung her head in shame. 'I wanted to help you. I thought that if I warned you about the bats, then you'd trust me. I thought I could get away with hiding the terrible truth from you. I'm so ashamed of what I once was, and of all of the despicable things I did. As soon as I was cured I swore I would spend the rest of my life stopping vampire bats from inflicting their evil on the world again.'

'How were you cured?' I asked, feeling hopeful.

'I don't know,' Sphinx said simply. I looked to the truth trout, hoping to see it go red and expose Sphinx as a liar. But it didn't.

'How can you not know?' the wish frog asked.

Sphinx shrugged and shook her head sadly. 'All I know is that one day I was swooping through the skies as a beast of the night. The next I was a cat again, and all of the other bats seemed to be cured too. I've been able to speak human languages since I was cured. I don't know how that happened either. Although there is one thing I do know . . .'

'What?' Donny, Red and I asked all at once.

'There was one vampire bat who wasn't cured. One vampire bat who had vanished once we were all turned back to what we once were.'

'Zoomanna?' Donny guessed.

Sphinx nodded.

'What else can you tell us about being a vampire bat?' the wish frog asked.

Sphinx told us everything she knew. She spoke for hours and hours. The truth trout shone a brilliant blue all the time she spoke, so we knew she was telling the truth. Sphinx was still talking long after the sun had set. My tummy rumbled but I didn't care how hungry I was. I just needed to know what we were dealing with.

Sammy Feral's Guide to
Vampire Bats

Chapter 1

* Weird vampire bats originated in Transylvania, but now they travel the world in search of prey.

* It takes several bites to turn a human child into a vampire bat, but other animals can be turned with just one bite.

* Colonies of vampire bats are led by a chief – Sphinx's chief was Zoomanna.

* The colony chiefs report to the Vampire Bat High Council, a mysterious organization that very little is known about.

* When a creature is turned into a
  vampire bat it lives an unnaturally
  long life.

* When vampire bats are cured and
  turned back into the creatures they
  once were – at the age they once
  were – they are sometimes left with
  weird powers (like Sphinx, who can
  now speak human languages).

So basically Natty, and every other child in my town, is slowly turning into a vampire bat. If we don't do something they'll soon sprout wings and fly away into the night.

That is not going to happen!

I took Sphinx back home with me from the zoo tonight. I thought keeping her nearby might be a good idea if the vampire bats come back, in case she can help in some way. She's under strict instructions not to mutter a word of English. I figured Mum wouldn't mind a stray cat staying for a couple of days – it's not like I've invited a yeti for tea again – but an English-speaking ex-vampire bat . . . no way! Plus, if Mum caught a whiff of what was going on with Natty, then she'd want to get involved. And it's way too dangerous. This kind of stuff is best left to the professionals.

Sphinx slurped up the last of the milk

I'd poured into a saucer on the kitchen floor. 'Where am I sleeping tonight?'

'You can have my bed,' I told her. 'But try to hide from my mum, just for tonight. I need to figure out what I'm going to tell her about you.'

'Where will you be sleeping?' Sphinx asked.

I gave her a mischievous smile. 'Sleep is for wimps.'

Most people would freak out if they discovered their sister was being turned into a vampire.

But not me. Oh no! Do you know why? Because I'm Sammy Feral, Master of Weird. There's no way the bats are having my sister, no way! I'll do anything to make sure she's safe.

The vampire bats will rue the day they decided to come to MY village!

I'm planning to sit up by Natty's bed all

night and fight off any bats that dare to come into her room.

I have drunk three cups of coffee (yuck!). I am armed with a cricket bat, a can of spray deodorant and a rolled-up newspaper and I am ready to FIGHT!

Any vampire bat that comes near Natty tonight will have me to answer to!

Tuesday 12th October

I stayed awake all night on the lookout for vampire bats. I didn't get a single minute of sleep, but my stake-out was a success. Not one bloodsucker in sight! If I can keep this up, then they'll never come near Natty again – result!

I'm SO tired though. School today is going to be horrible!

Wednesday 13th October

I was way too weary to write anything else in my diary yesterday.

I have not slept for two whole nights. I've sat guard by Natty's bed to protect her from vampire bats. Yesterday at school I told Tommy, Katrina and everyone else with kid siblings to do the same.

'Beware the vampire bats,' I whispered in Katrina's ear as we were queuing up in the lunch hall today.

'Maybe you should get some sleep,' Katrina said kindly. 'There's no such thing as vampire bats. You sound crazy.'

'Crazy?' I said, my tired eyes bulging from my head. 'I'm not crazy! What's crazy is that you don't want to help your sister. If you don't watch out for the vampire bats, then they'll turn her into one of them!'

'Sammy, I think you should—'

'VAMPIRE ATTACK!' I shouted at the top of my voice. I ran and jumped on to a nearby table, kicking a boy's soup out of the way. I stamped my feet and waved my arms about so I got everyone's attention. Soon the whole school fell silent, stopped eating their lunch and looked at me like I'd just painted myself purple and sprouted feathers.

'Beware the bats!' I shouted, waving my arms about wildly. 'Those of you with kid brothers and sisters – you need to protect them. They're all being turned into vampire bats! Don't sleep, don't eat – you shouldn't even be at school. We should all be at home . . .'

I felt someone tugging on my trouser leg. I looked down and saw Mark staring up at me. 'Sammy, I think you should get down from the table.'

'But I need to warn everyone about the bats!'

'They heard you, mate, they heard you. Loud and clear.'

Mark helped me down and people started laughing as he led me out of the dining hall. 'You sound like a maniac,' he said as we walked into an empty corridor.

'I'm not mad!' I told him. 'You believe me. You know as well as I do that weird animals exist. Just because you're an only child doesn't mean you shouldn't worry about everyone else's brothers and sisters.'

'I'm worried about you, Sammy! You need to sleep. As soon as school's over you should go home and get some rest.'

'Can't,' I said, my eyes twitching manically. 'I have chores at the zoo and I have to spend tonight watching over Natty again. I can't let the bats get her!'

The rest of the day passed in a blur. I think Mark might be right. I think the lack of sleep is starting to affect me. I keep laughing at things that aren't funny – like when I was sweeping out the sloth bears at the zoo after school and I saw a piece of straw that looked like a nose. I laughed so hard I started to cry. That is not normal behaviour.

Luckily Mum and Dad are too worried about the state of the zoo to notice just how crazy I'm acting. The Zoo of the Year judges are coming to Feral Zoo this weekend, so we're in a race against the clock to get everything spick and span.

I had to stay at the zoo until gone ten o'clock this evening, helping to clean the railings by the flamingo lake. I was so busy with zoo chores that I didn't even have a chance to go Backstage and tell Donny and Red how successful my vampire-bat protection plan is.

But I am SO tired! I think I must have fallen asleep standing up, because one minute I was polishing a metal railing and the next I was leaning against it face first.

I walked home with a streak of black polish all the way down my face.

11 P.M.

I am sitting on the floor by Natty's bed, trying to stay awake. She's asleep under the covers. Her skin is as pale as snow. Mum said she hasn't eaten any food in four days. The only nutrition she's had is some blood sucked out of raw steaks. Gross! Luckily Mum just thinks it's a weird werewolf hangover. I don't understand . . . I've been watching out for vampire bats every night. Nothing's bitten her in days. Why is she still so ill?

P.S. Mum hasn't even noticed that Sphinx is living with us. Sphinx has spent the last two days in my bedroom, reading my books on big cats and coming and going as she pleases through my bedroom window. Not sure what she's been eating. I haven't been feeding her. I have other things to worry about. Like where all the vampire bats have gone, whether Natty will get better and how I can stop myself from falling asl . . .

1 A.M.

I must have nodded off for a moment, but there's no sign that the bats came back so I think we're safe. I'm fighting to stay awake. I've reread every page in my diary to stop myself falling asleep. (I really have had some amazing adventures!)

2 A.M.

I think I heard a noise outside. I'm trying to stay . . .

Thursday 14th October

I haven't felt this guilty since the time I accidentally stepped on a hickory horned caterpillar in the butterfly enclosure.

How could I have let myself fall asleep last night?

I woke up this morning and the bruise on Natty's neck looks worse than ever. The vampire bats must have returned in the night, and I was too busy sleeping to stop them feeding off my little sister!

'I'm so, so sorry, Natty,' I whispered as I stood over her bed this morning. 'I'll try harder to protect you tonight, I promise.'

The only good thing to come out of sleeping for a few hours last night is that I don't feel as tired as I did yesterday. I quickly took a shower and brushed my teeth before throwing on my school uniform and heading downstairs for breakfast.

'Miaoww,' said a small voice from underneath the kitchen table.

'We've adopted a stray cat,' Grace announced. 'I've been feeding her milk for days now. I don't think she has an owner, so she's going to come and live here.'

I didn't need to look under the table to know just which cat I'd find there.

'Sphinx, come out here now!' I demanded.

Sphinx's black face emerged from underneath the kitchen table and she smiled up at me.

'I did wonder how you were feeding yourself. I see my sister's taken pity on you.'

'Sphinx?' Grace asked.

'Is my name,' Sphinx said. Grace looked around the room, confused about where the voice was coming from.

I quickly checked that Mum and Dad were nowhere in earshot. 'Sphinx isn't an ordinary cat. She's a weird cat.'

'Hey, less of the weird, please!' Sphinx protested.

'She can . . . can . . . speak?' Grace gasped, her eyes darting towards Sphinx and nearly popping clean out of her head.

'I don't know why that should surprise *you*, Grace.' I rolled my eyes. 'You're an ex-werewolf.'

'Sammy has kindly agreed that I can stay here.' Sphinx smirked up at Grace. 'Although I believe your parents aren't yet aware of our arrangement.'

Grace looked down at Sphinx, her mouth nearly scraping the floor in shock. 'I don't think Mum would mind too much if we adopted a stray cat, but if she knew you were a speaking cat . . .'

'Best we keep that little secret among ourselves then.' Sphinx narrowed her eyes.

Keeping secrets from my parents. Fending off vampire bats. Trying to save my little sister from certain doom.

Why is my life *always* so complicated?

Friday 15th October

'So let me get this right.' Grace pushed her hair out of her eyes with the back of her hand. We were mucking out the warthogs at the zoo after school. 'Vampire bats exist. They travel from town to town infecting children by feeding from them.'

'Their saliva is mega-contagious,' I nodded, shovelling poo into a slop bag.

'They feed from the children every night,' she continued, 'and eventually the children turn into vampire bats and just disappear? Where do they go once they've turned?'

I shrugged, pausing mid-poo scoop and

thinking. 'Maybe once people turn into vampires they want to get as far away from their home as possible, to stop themselves from attacking their family.'

'Speaking of attacking family . . .' Grace threw her broom to the ground and looked up at the sky, which was growing darker. The nearly full moon was peeking out from behind dark clouds. 'I need to go home and get ready for the full moon. There's no way I want anyone at the zoo to watch my ear hair get out of control as soon as the sun sets.'

It's mega-unlucky that the Zoo of the Year inspection has been scheduled for the full moon. Dad tried to rearrange it but the competition organizers wouldn't let him. It means I'm going to have to host the inspection, because none of my family can be at the zoo when the judges are here. The sight of my mum eating one of the lions' raw steaks probably wouldn't score us any points.

'You'll have to finish up the rest of the zoo chores on your own, Sammy,' Grace said, taking off her thick gloves and throwing them to the ground. 'Good luck.'

I watched my big sister walk off. The moon was getting brighter in the sky and any moment now she'd start to show signs of her inner wolf.

It's not as bad as it used to be — not since I invented a cure for werewolves. But excessive ear hair, a need for raw meat and a mega-grouchy attitude are symptoms they're going to always have to live with.

After I'd finished mucking out the warthogs I polished all the zoo signs and swept the leaves from the zoo entrance. Feral Zoo is looking as shiny as the back of a glistening toad.

When the judges arrive tomorrow we've got a good chance of scoring some mega-high points. The only thing that worries me is the Backstage area — I hope they don't want to inspect that. I'm not sure how I'd explain a phoenix, a gut worm, a fire-breathing turtle and a truth trout.

Being responsible for showing the Zoo of the Year judges around the zoo is quite stressful. If anything goes wrong, then I'll get the blame and when we don't win it will be my fault. How crud-tacular is that?!

But I'm quite pleased to have it as a distraction at the moment. It stops me thinking about vampire bats.

Because every time I think about vampire bats I get this horrible hollow feeling in the pit of my stomach. It feels like I'm standing on the edge of a cliff, looking down and waiting to fall. Natty might not be getting any worse, but she's not getting better. The vampire bats might be lying dormant at the moment, but they'll be back – I'm sure they will.

Donny and Red seem more interested in fighting off hissing hinkypinks than in helping me, Sphinx is about as helpful as a winking wildebeest, and my entire family are about to sprout ear hair and howl at the moon for three nights.

I'm all on my own.

But I will not be broken! Oh no. I'm Sammy Feral – a weird warrior with an arsenal of crypto-fighting skills – and it takes more than a few bitey bats to scare me.

I am flexing my muscles as I write this – I am ready to FIGHT!

Saturday 16th October

7 A.M.

I am at the zoo mega-early to make sure everything is in tip-top shape for the judges.

After I had finished clearing fish guts out of the penguin tanks, the zoo looks as sparkly as shimmering shark fins.

Bring this inspection on!

11 A.M.

Zoo of the Year judges = stuck-up dinosaurs with more grease in their hair than an oil tanker!

'But you're just a scabby-kneed schoolboy!'

snarled the chief judge, looking me up and down.

Er, I'm wearing long trousers today (it's mega-cold outside) so how does he even know my knees are scabby?

'Where are your parents? We wish to be shown around the zoo by Mr and Mrs Feral.'

'Mr and Mrs Feral are indisposed,' I said in my most grown-up voice. I learned the word 'indisposed' in English last term and thought that using it would impress them. 'And they wanted to take this opportunity to show you the strength of their apprentice programme here at Feral Zoo. I'm a zoo-keeping apprentice, and I know just as much as they do.'

My plan obviously worked because after a short pause the man said, 'Well, come on then. Let's get this over with.'

So I spent the next two hours showing the Zoo of the Year judges around the zoo.

From the snoozing Sumatran tigers to the lip-
smacking llamas, I gave them a
very thorough tour.

At every animal
enclosure they stopped
to scribble notes on
their official Zoo of
the Year clipboards.
And I made sure we
stopped off in the zoo
cafe so they could try
the delicious sandwiches
and cakes that we had on
sale (I quickly wolfed down
some banana bread – yum!). Every now and
again one of them would murmur something
to another one, who would nod in agreement.
I couldn't tell whether the murmurs were good
or bad. But I kept my fingers crossed behind my
back the whole time, just in case.

143

I tried to answer every question they asked me in my grown-up voice. 'Yes, the lions are only fed organic, free-range meat . . . Yes, we have the largest giraffe enclosure in Europe . . . No, we don't let the zoo visitors pet the hyenas . . . Of course the giant sea turtles have a breeding programme – we hatched 50 baby turtles last year alone.'

It was all going really well until we came to the Backstage gate . . .

'And what's behind here?' asked one woman whose hair was slicked into a sharp side parting, making her look like some kind of greasy robot.

I panicked. 'Umm . . . let's move on.'

The chief judge grabbed me by the shoulder and pulled me back. 'Not so fast, young man. We're here to inspect every nook and cranny of the zoo. We need to see behind this gate.'

Er, major dilemma!

I had no idea what to do. Refuse to let the

inspectors Backstage and ruin the zoo's chances of winning Zoo of the Year? Or let them in and expose them to the freak show in the Backstage offices?

I opened my mouth, unsure of what I was going to say, when the Backstage door swung open and Donny came waltzing out. 'Sammy —' he grinned from ear to ear — 'I was hoping to see you today. We need to have a serious chat about vampire b—'

'Books!' I interrupted him. 'Vampire books. I hate them, don't you?' I asked the judges in panic. 'This is Donny, one of our specialist zookeepers. Donny, these are the judges for Zoo of the Year. I'm . . .'

Before I could finish my sentence the chief inspector barged past Donny and through the Backstage gates. The other inspectors followed.

Yikes!

My heart started beating at the speed of a

charging cheetah. 'Donny!' I whispered through clenched teeth, pushing him back through the gate and following the judges. 'This is not good. We cannot let them see what's going on back here!'

'Why?' Donny asked, confused.

Donny may be a brilliant cryptozoologist, but he can be as daft as a dozy dart frog sometimes!

'Your pets!' I exclaimed, running after the inspectors as they quickly made their way towards the Backstage offices. 'We can't let them see your pets.'

'The door's locked,' muttered the chief judge in frustration as he rattled the knob. 'I demand to see inside.'

My grown-up voice vanished and I sounded like a scared kid as I said, 'Um, I don't think that's a good idea.'

'Allow me,' Donny smiled, slipping a key into the lock.

Blood rushed to my head. I felt as if I was hanging upside down on a giant roller coaster! What was Donny doing?

My parents have dedicated their whole lives to Feral Zoo. They'd lose everything in a heartbeat if the truth about Backstage ever came out. How was I ever going to explain the sight of a phoenix?

A genetic mutation?

A clever robot?

A hologram?

All these ideas whizzed through my head as I walked into the Backstage offices and prepared to lie through my teeth at the sight of Donny's pet collection.

But there was nothing to see.

Nothing at all.

No crazy creatures, no books on vampire bats, nothing.

There was just Red, sitting in the middle of the room reading a book called *The Zookeepers' Guide to Lion Taming*.

'Panda snot,' Donny whispered to me.

Of course! Panda snot can turn things invisible!

I could have burst into song and danced the cha-cha, I was so happy! Donny had covered everything with panda snot, hiding it all from the inspectors.

'This is where the zookeepers come to catch up on reading and have a cup of well-earned tea.' Donny smiled at the judges. 'Would you like one?'

'No,' the chief judge snarled. 'We've seen everything we need to. We'll write up our report and submit it to the committee. You'll be hearing from us shortly.'

9 P.M.

After the judges left I whizzed around the zoo catching up on chores. I still have to fill in for my family and Max as the moon is full. Dad's told the other zookeepers that they have to go away once a month to work on a wolf-conservation project. No one has a clue that he's lying.

Once all the zoo chores were done I went Backstage to catch up with Donny and Red about the vampire-bat situation. We carefully washed the panda snot off all the crypto-pets, so we could see them again. As I scrubbed the snot off the gut worm's cage I described how I'd tried to stay awake to protect Natty.

'. . . I did everything I could, but I think

the bats still managed to find their way in while I was sleeping. So what should we do now?' I asked.

'There's not much we can do unless the bats appear again. And the best thing for you to do, Sammy, is speak to them.'

'Er, have you gone crazy? Why would I speak to a vampire bat?'

'Because you can. You're the only one of us who has a chance of understanding their language. We know there's a way to cure them – Sphinx is proof of that – but we need to figure out how. And who knows, if they can't be cured then maybe they'll be willing to negotiate. There's no harm in trying.'

It was already dark as I walked back through the zoo, thinking hard about how on earth I was ever going to manage to have a conversation with a vampire bat. I hadn't seen the bats hanging around my house for days (thank goodness!), so how was I even meant to find one?

They don't just fall out of the sky!

SWOOP! WHOOSH! ZOOM!

At that moment a giant vampire bat appeared in the sky.

Two vampire bats, to be precise.

They swooped down through the air above me, heading for a nearby tree.

This was my chance!

The two bats landed on a low branch and then swung themselves upside down, hanging by just their toes. Such a cool trick.

Their backs were turned so they didn't see me approach, and the wind was howling pretty loudly in my direction so their super-sensitive hearing didn't seem to pick up the sound of my footsteps as I came towards them. I was just about to open my mouth and try out my best Vampire Bat accent, when the sound of a high-pitched voice was carried towards me on the breeze.

'Where is everyone? Have we got the right day for the meeting?'

Excuse me . . . what meeting? What were they talking about?

It didn't take a genius to work out that any meeting involving vampire bats was probably top secret and not something they'd want to tell me about. So I hid in the shadows and stayed as still as I could, careful not to make a sound, so I could eavesdrop on their conversation.

'You're right,' said the second vampire bat. 'If it was the right day, we wouldn't be able to move for bats.'

Rewind! What kind of meeting would involve thousands of vampire bats?

'I'm surprised more of us didn't get it wrong. The instructions from the High Council weren't very straightforward: Feral Zoo flamingo pond, midnight of the full moon.'

The Vampire Bat High Council . . . here at Feral Zoo . . . ?

Why didn't I like the sound of that? *'Well the moon's only full for another night – so it must be tomorrow night instead.'*

'So let's come back then.'

The two bats let go of the branch and swooped up into the air with a lightning-fast beat of their wings. I stayed hidden in the shadows, watching them disappear into the night.

Oh. My. Giddy giddy gosh.

Wow.

I can't believe what I've just heard.

There's a meeting of the Vampire Bat High Council here at Feral Zoo tomorrow night.

I have to find a way to be there!

Sunday 17th October

'This is as bad as a rotten crocodile tooth!' I held my head in my hands as Sphinx finished telling us all she knew about the Vampire Bat High Council.

The Vampire Bat High Council – Top Five Facts

1) Every colony of vampire bats has a chief, and every colony chief reports to the Vampire Bat High Council.

2) They make a ritual sacrifice at every meeting.

3) No human being has ever attended a meeting and survived.

4) The chief of all chiefs, and the head of the High Council, is the evil Count Batula.

5) They show no mercy.

I was Backstage with Donny, Red, Sphinx and the wish frog, and I'd quickly filled them in on everything I'd overheard the night before. Things were looking bad, and one thing was really playing on my mind . . . 'You didn't think to tell us ANY of this before?' I asked Sphinx angrily. 'You promised you'd tell us everything you knew!'

'I told you everything I thought was important. I had no idea the Vampire Bat High Council was mixed up in any of this. The Vampire Bat High Council is one of the most mysterious organizations in the world. I've never known another bat who's been to a meeting. The council live in a lair in Transylvania – they don't fly around like normal vampire bats. That's what the colonies are for, to do their dirty work,' Sphinx purred. 'As far as I know, the council only leave their lair in times of great emergency.'

'What do you think the emergency is?' asked the wish frog.

'Who knows?' Red shrugged. 'But one thing's for certain, we can't be anywhere near the zoo this evening. Not unless we want to be rounded up and ritually sacrificed to Count Batula!'

'What are you talking about?' I asked, flabbergasted. 'We HAVE to be at the zoo tonight. We HAVE to know what they're meeting about, and why they've chosen Feral Zoo. How else are we ever going to stop them from turning children into vampire bats?'

'On this occasion I'd have to agree with you, Sammy.' Donny nodded. 'We all need to be at that meeting. Otherwise we'll never get to the bottom of the vampire bats' evil plans.'

Red shot me a gaze that could have frozen

dragon breath. I could tell she was super-annoyed, but Red never argues with Donny. 'And how exactly are we supposed to sneak in undetected?'

'Panda snot.' Donny grinned. 'We'll cover ourselves from head to toe and they'll never see us.'

'But they'll hear us,' said the wish frog wisely. 'Bats have the most extraordinary sense of hearing.'

'Well, you're a wish frog,' Sphinx said in a super-smooth voice. 'I wish for us to make no sound this evening.'

The wish frog's eyes bulged from his head and his tiny face turned a violent shade of scarlet. 'I AM RETIRED FROM WISH GRANTING!'

'No need to shout,' Sphinx grunted.

'It's simple,' Donny said, raising his palms to try to calm everyone down. 'All we need to do is make sure we're at the flamingo pond before sunset. We'll be there long before midnight. If we're there before the bats, then they won't hear us arrive. And we just need to be extra careful that we don't make a single sound. No talking. No sneezing. No coughing. No laughing. And no matter what happens, no matter how bad the situation is . . . no screaming.'

Watch a vampire-bat ritual sacrifice and not scream? What am I meant to do — stuff a pair of stinking socks in my mouth? Freeze-blast my throat? Fit myself with a werewolf muzzle?

Something tells me this is going to be one long, tough night!

7 P.M.

I am covered from head to toe in panda snot. It's dripping on to the page and I'm worried I soon won't be able to see my diary to write in! Donny is putting the last few snotty touches to Sphinx and then we'll all be invisible.

We're about to go down to the flamingo pond.

I'm so nervous, I feel as if I'm going to puke.

If I never write in my diary again, it will be because I've been offered up to Count Batula as a ritual sacrifice and torn limb from limb by a swarm of evil vampire bats!

11 P.M.

We took up our positions just before sunset. Invisible with panda snot, we hid in plain sight, waiting for the vampire bats to descend on Feral Zoo.

'How long are we going to have to wait?' I whispered.

'As long as it takes,' Donny replied. 'Now, not another word, Sammy. We can't risk the bats detecting us. Their hearing is so good they could hear us talking from miles away. If they know we're here, then we're all done for.'

Doh!

What was I thinking?

Talking, even in whispers, was as stupid as a samba-dancing squirrel.

No way was I risking that again!

We crouched in silence for what felt like hours. The light faded and the air grew colder. I tried my hardest not to even shiver – I couldn't risk the bats picking up on the sound of my chattering teeth!

I was just beginning to think that the bats I heard had been wrong and the meeting had been cancelled when the first vampire bat arrived.

It swooped down out of the shadows and landed on a nearby branch. Its beady eyes glowed coal-red in the darkness, and the moonlight bounced off its razor-sharp fangs.

Was this one of the vampire bats who had been sinking his teeth into my sister's neck? Just the thought of it made me want to rip the branch off the tree, capture the evil bat and lock it up in a damp, dark prison for the rest of eternity. I clenched my fists and tried to remain as cool as an alley cat . . . now was not the time to lose control.

The first vampire bat was quickly joined by a second, then a third and a fourth. Soon the night sky was alive with the sight and sound of thousands of bat wings, and they were all coming down to land in Feral Zoo.

I held my breath. It was almost too much effort not to scream. These were the most powerful vampire bats in the world. Who knew how much death and destruction they were responsible for! All I wanted to do was burst out of my hiding place and take down every furry-faced critter in my path.

'*SILENCE!*' boomed a voice in the Vampire Bat language.

Instantly the rustling of bat wings and the sound of excited bat chatter fell away and all I could hear was the wind in my ears.

I watched as a crowd of bats parted to make way for one giant bat that flew among them.

He was twice the size of all the others. His wings were stained blood-red, like a cloak around his body. Giant knife-sharp fangs protruded on either side of his mouth and his tiny beady eyes shone red like fire in the darkness.

I recognized him instantly.

It was the very same bat I'd seen in Natty's room – the bat who had told me he would come for me next.

I bit down on my tongue, trying hard not to scream.

It was him – their chief of chiefs.

Count Batula.

'Silence, minions,' he said, even though the other vampire bats were already silent. 'I have summoned you here this night, under the light of the full moon, to inform you all that our plans have changed.'

'But what about world domination?' shouted a bat from deep within the crowd. 'What about drowning the moon in blood and watching the oceans and rivers run red?'

'SILENCE!' Count Batula roared. 'I wish for

no minions to speak. Only the sound of my voice shall ring out this night. You are here to listen. You are here to obey my command. Do not question the great wisdom of the mighty Count Batula!'

Jeez, this guy was as arrogant as a peacock in a parade!

'We will still strive for world domination. One by one we will turn the children of this earth into creatures of the night. The moon will drown in the blood of the innocent. The rivers and seas will run red as we turn each mewling child into one of us. But there has been a glitch in our mighty plan. A single boy — Sammy Feral — is foolish enough to think he can stop us! Well, HE CANNOT!' Count Batula shouted this last bit, and large flecks of spit frothed at the side of his mouth and his eyes bulged as he spoke.

He knows my name . . . He knows my name . . . He knows MY NAME . . .

I tried not to panic. The most powerful

bat EVER had me in his sights. I swear I felt a trickle of sweat drip down my face . . . I swear the bats should have heard . . .

Good job I was invisible – my chances of taking on a thousand angry vampire bats and winning were a big fat zero!

'But we are mighty vampire bats. We will not give up. We will not relent. Nothing can hold us back from our true destiny. Nothing will stop us from RULING THE WHOLE WORLD! But we need to be stronger. We need to swell our forces. And we shall do that now . . . here . . . tonight!'

Now? Here? Tonight?

'Mwahahahahahahaaaa!' Count Batula erupted into manic evil laughter, and as he did so the other vampire bats around him joined in. The air filled with the sound of thousands of excited vampire bats, cackling wildly and flapping their wings in deranged delight, hungry for blood.

'I GATHERED YOU ALL HERE TONIGHT,' Count Batula roared over the sound of flapping wings, *'SO YOU COULD MAKE A SACRIFICE TO THE VAMPIRE BAT HIGH COUNCIL. But you will not just sacrifice one life, oh no. Tonight you will sacrifice every animal in this zoo.'*

W.H.A.T??

No, no, please – not the zoo animals!

My heart fell into the floor. I'm sure if the bats weren't so unhinged with excitement they could have heard it.

'Here, tonight,' Count Batula continued, his eyes blazing with evil exhilaration, *'we will rise up and deliver the creatures of this zoo to a glorious destiny. We will sink our fangs deep in their necks and turn them into vampire bats. The light of the full moon means that we only need one bite – our powers are heightened and our prey will be turned with just one drop of our saliva! Once the animals of the zoo have become vampire bats, they will*

remember nothing of their life before. All they will know is the thirst for blood, the desire to bite all innocent children – the desire to TAKE OVER THE EARTH!

'*Every lion, every tiger, every anteater, antelope and otter. Every spider, every toad. The camels, koalas, chameleons and cats, the fleas that live on the backs of the cats – nothing shall be spared!*'

The bats erupted into screeches of delight. Without thinking, I covered my ears with my hands – the noise was deafening.

'They're planning to turn all the animals in the zoo into vampire bats!' I quickly told the others. I had to hope the sound of the screeching bats was so loud they'd never hear me whisper, even with their super-sensitive hearing.

'When?' Red whispered, panic in her voice.

'*NOW!*' commanded Count Batula.

There was no need for me to translate as the vampire bats swarmed up into the air.

I felt an invisible hand reach out and grab hold of my arm. It was Red. She pulled me towards her and Donny, and together, with the wish frog and Sphinx between us, we all huddled close in terror.

The sound of thousands of bats whooshing through the night made my eardrums feel like bursting. I scrunched my eyes shut. I didn't want to see what was happening. There was nothing I could do. We had no power to stop it. Every single animal in Feral Zoo was going to be turned into a vampire bat!

Every. Last. One.

Monday 18th October

Feral Zoo is closed until further notice due to an outbreak of deadly bat flu.

Dad hung the sign on the zoo gate first thing this morning.

'Every animal,' Mum whispered, her face drained of blood. Anyone would think that *she* had been attacked by vampires. 'Not one of them was spared?'

I was standing by the empty elephant enclosure with Mum, Dad, Grace, Donny, Red and Sphinx. Natty was at home in bed, still too weak to leave the house.

'So every animal in the zoo is now a vampire bat?' Dad said in horror.

I nodded.

'And . . . Natty . . . could be next?' Mum said, her eyes filling with tears.

'Along with every other child in the village,' Red explained, without a shred of sympathy for my mum. I shot Red an angry stare but she ignored me and carried on. 'And not only in this village, but in every village, town and city in the world. The vampire bats won't stop until every last child on earth has been turned.'

Mum turned to me, eyes blazing. 'Once again you have failed to tell us that we were all in mortal danger, Sammy.'

'How could I tell you?' I said, trying to defend myself. 'I knew you'd freak out and try to go after the vampire bats. I didn't want to put you in danger. Besides . . .' I trailed off, 'I thought I could handle it.'

'Well, you've not done a very good job at handling things so far,' Mum said angrily, pointing to the empty animal enclosure. I HATED it when she was right like this! 'Is there anything else you've neglected to mention?'

'He hasn't told you that I can speak,' Sphinx purred.

Trust Sphinx to make a bad situation worse!

'Sammy Feral,' Mum said, staring at the cat in wonder, 'just you wait until—'

'Never mind about grounding me, Mum,' I cut in. 'Right now we need a plan. We can't let the vampire bats do any more damage. Maybe there's even a way we can cure the zoo animals of being vampire bats.'

'You're right, Sammy,' Donny said, matter-of-fact. 'This isn't the first time we've been faced with certain doom. Everyone – you know what to do. It's battle stations!'

Everyone gathered around and
Donny dished out jobs . . .

* Mum and Dad –
  Find a way to get
  the zoo up and
  running again
* Grace – Stay
  with Natty, nurse
  her back to health
* Wish Frog – Stay safe.
  We can't risk him being turned into a
  vampire bat
* Sphinx – Keep out of Mum's way. She's
  not too keen on having a talking cat
  around!
* Donny and Red – Track down the
  vampire bats so that we can cure them
* Me – Find a cure

Why do I always get the impossible jobs?!

Tuesday 19th October

Sammy Feral = the boy who discovered the cure for the werewolf virus.

If I can find a cure for werewolves, then surely I can find one for vampire bats! How hard can it be?

I've borrowed Donny's books on vampires and I've fired up the Internet.

Research! Research! Research!

I won't rest until I've found the cure.

The only problem is that every book and every website I look at says there is no cure. Once someone has been turned into a vampire bat, then there's no going back. The only way to stop them being a vampire bat is to kill them. And the only ways to kill a vampire are:

* Exposure to sunlight
* A wooden stake through the heart
* Decapitation
* Holy water

Killing all the vampire bats isn't an option.

We want the children and zoo animals back in one piece, not blasted into vampire dust with a wooden stake.

Besides, we know for a fact that there is a cure. Sphinx was cured – she just can't remember how. So stuff the research, the books and the Internet – I'm as clueless as a cricket in a cornfield.

What am I going to do?!

Wednesday 20th October

I'd rather be eaten alive by a pack of rabid rabbits than not find a cure for vampire bats.

Mum cornered me as soon as I stepped into the house after school today. 'She's getting worse.'

I threw down my school bag and took the stairs two at a time.

I froze in Natty's bedroom doorway, my heart skipping a beat at the sight of my little sister.

She was lying in her bed, shivering under the covers. Her skin looked like cold marble and her eyes stared up at the ceiling without blinking. Grace was sitting beside her on the bed, holding her hand and weeping quietly. 'She's dying, Sammy,' Grace sniffed without looking at me.

'She's not dying,' I tried to reassure her. 'She's just turning into a vampire bat.'

Grace spun around. Her eyes were red and puffy. '*Just* turning into a vampire? Same thing as dying! I thought you said the vampire bats hadn't visited her in a while.'

'Maybe it's the full moon?' I said weakly. 'Count Batula said that it heightened their powers. Maybe it's strengthening the venom in Natty's system.'

'Time is running out,' Grace said gravely.

She was right.

Looking at Natty, it's a miracle she hasn't already taken to the skies.

How long have I got before I lose her forever?

Thursday 21st October

Dear Feral Zoo,
CONGRATULATIONS!
The Zoo of the Year committee are delighted to inform you that you have been selected as the winner of this year's Zoo of the Year award. Our team of judges were greatly impressed with Feral Zoo's wide range of animals and the standard to which your animals are housed and cared for. It was fantastic to be shown around the zoo by one of your youngest zookeepers – we found it very reassuring that Feral Zoo has such a successful training programme for apprentices.

As is the Zoo of the Year custom, we shall hold an award ceremony at your zoo. The award ceremony will be on Sunday 31st October.

Please ensure that you make all the necessary arrangements.

We look forward to seeing you then and presenting you with your award.

Yours sincerely,
The Zoo of the Year committee

'What are we going to do?' Mum clapped her hands to her face in horror. 'We only have ten days until 31st October!'

'That's Halloween,' I thought aloud. 'Aren't we going to be busy fighting off hissing hinkypinks, grouchy gremlins and any other weird animal that comes our way?'

'We can't have an award ceremony here!' Mum continued. 'We don't even have any animals! They've all been turned into vampire bats!'

That was a very, very good point.

There was no way we could explain the disappearance of every animal in Feral Zoo!

'Don't worry, Mum,' I said with A LOT more confidence than I felt. 'I'm working on a way to cure vampire bats. By Halloween all the animals will be back in their enclosures and as good as new.'

'Never mind the animals,' Grace chimed in.

'What about Natty? She's worse than ever. It's only a matter of time before she's flapping about with bat wings.'

'Trust me,' I reassured them all. 'I have it all under control.'

Sammy Feral = big fat liar.

I have nothing under control, not really. We only have ten days until the Zoo of the Year ceremony, and if the animals aren't back by then we may as well all pack our bags and run away with the circus, because Feral Zoo will never be able to open its doors again.

But Grace is right, even worse than the fate of the zoo is the state of Natty.

She doesn't look like she even has ten days left.

Time is running out.

Fast.

Friday 22nd October
9 days until Halloween

Natty has disappeared.

This morning her bed
was empty and her
bedroom curtains were
flapping in the breeze.

Mum hasn't
stopped crying.
Dad won't speak
to anyone. Grace
refuses to face up
to the truth – she's
searching under the

sofa, inside the fridge and behind the TV, trying to find Natty.

But Natty's nowhere to be found.

We need to accept the chilling truth.

It's finally happened.

She's turned into a vampire bat.

Saturday 23rd October
8 days until Halloween

Natty's not the only child in our village who's disappeared. Every other child under the age of ten has vanished without a trace. Tommy's brother, Katrina's sister — not one has been spared.

They've all gone.

No one can find them. Not their parents. Not the police. Not even the TV and newspaper crews that have descended on Tyler's Rest since word got out. There's not a clue to go on. They've all simply vanished.

Only a few of us know the terrible truth.

My little sister now has fangs and wings and wants to suck the blood out of every living creature she comes across.

The thought makes me as sick as the stench of a hissing hinkypink fresh out of the sewer.

Last night there was an emergency meeting in the village hall. Everyone was there – the families of the missing children, the schoolteachers, the police and the news crews.

'Children don't just vanish into thin air!' one woman yelled, her face stained with tears. 'It's impossible.'

'What's impossible,' another woman shouted, 'is that this is the second time this has happened. Everyone remembers Barren Heath – the children vanished from there and haven't been seen since!'

The village hall erupted into shouts and cries.

It was horrible. The sight of so many crying mums and dads was one of the worst things I've ever seen – and I've seen some terrible sights in my time. But yeti kisses, Hell Hound curses, werewolf drool and dragon fire were a walk in the park compared to this.

Donny, Red and I stood at the back of the hall.

'We have to do something,' I muttered under my breath.

'We *are* doing something,' Donny muttered back. 'We're doing everything we can to track down the bats.'

'Any luck with that?' I asked hopefully.

Red and Donny both shook their heads. 'And it's nearly Halloween,' Donny pointed out. 'Every day we're getting more and more reports of weird animal sightings. Apparently the sewers of London are overrun with hissing hinkypinks. We can't ignore an outbreak like that . . .'

'Nothing's more important than finding the vampire bats!' I hissed through gritted teeth. 'I'd fight a million hissing hinkypinks single-handed if it meant getting my sister back.'

'If we don't stop the hissing hinkypink outbreak, then you might have to,' Red grumbled.

Can my life get any worse?

We have no idea where the vampire bats are hiding out.

And no idea how to cure them even if we do find them.

All we have to go on is the fact that Sphinx was once a vampire bat and was somehow cured.

It feels as hopeless as a mole without a hole.

I just want my sister back, that's all.

I'm prepared to do anything to save her.

Anything.

Sunday 24th October
7 days until Halloween

Ideas of how to get Natty back and cure her:

* Put out an ultrasonic screech sound to drive all vampire bats into the open

* Go undercover, a.ka. become a vampire bat and bring them down from the inside

* Kidnap a vampire bat and torture it for information.

'Letting yourself get turned into a vampire bat is one of the stupidest things you've ever suggested,' Red said, shaking her head. We were sitting around the Backstage kitchen table

with Donny, trying to figure
out some kind of plan.

'It worked for
Sphinx. She was a
vampire bat and lived
to tell the tale . . .
somehow. Have you
thought of anything
better?' I snapped.
'Because from where
I'm sitting it looks
like you've done a big fat
nothing.'

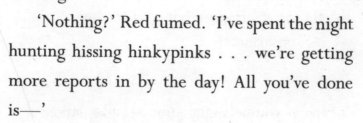

'Nothing?' Red fumed. 'I've spent the night
hunting hissing hinkypinks . . . we're getting
more reports in by the day! All you've done
is—'

'Calm down,' Donny said, raising his hand.
'We need to work together. And we need a plan.'
He looked at the list I'd written and scratched

his head in thought. 'I quite like the ultrasonic-screech idea. But if we're going to drive all the vampire bats out into the open, then we need to have some idea of what to do next.'

'You mean we need a cure,' Red cut in, looking at me menacingly. 'A cure that Sammy was meant to have come up with.'

'I'm working on it!' I growled.

'Now, this idea is interesting,' Donny said thoughtfully, pointing to the last idea on the list.

'The only problem with that,' I said quickly, 'is that even though it was my idea, I don't think I could ever torture anything, even a vampire bat.'

'I agree,' said Donny. 'Torturing is a definite no. But if we did manage to get our hands on a member of the Vampire Bat High Council, then maybe a little gentle persuasion . . .'

'So now all we need is a plan to kidnap a

member of the Vampire Bat High Council,' Red said, 'one of the most mysterious and deadly organizations in the world. How will we ever have a leaping leapfrog's chance of doing that?'

'Bait,' said a smooth voice from the corner of the room.

We all spun around to see Sphinx calmly trotting towards us.

'Count Batula is looking to swell his numbers. He wants more blood. We need to make him think that's what he's getting.'

'She's right,' Donny said. 'It's our only way in.'

Vampire-bat bait?

What, or who, are we going to use . . . ?

Monday 25th October
6 days until Halloween

8 P.M.

I didn't go to school today. I didn't help out around the zoo. And for once in my life my mum didn't give me a blasting. She's just pleased I'm alive. Although I may not be alive for much longer. This is why . . .

Sammy Feral = vampire-bat bait.

Last night, after I'd eaten my dinner and everyone had gone to bed, this text appeared on my phone:

OUTSIDE

That was my cue to sneak downstairs and let

in Donny, Red and the wish frog. I opened the door and looked out into the dark back garden. There was no sign of anyone there.

'Donny? Red?' I whispered into the night.

I felt something brush past me, and then I heard Red's voice say, 'Shut the door, Sammy, it's freezing out there.'

Huh?

'We're wearing panda snot,' came Donny's voice. 'Thought it would be easier to snare a bat if we were all invisible.'

I shut the back door. 'Good idea. Have you got everything we need?'

'We've brought a butterfly net and a small travel cage from the zoo,' Red whispered. 'They're also covered in panda snot, obviously.'

I led them upstairs as silently as I could. 'So how do we tempt a vampire bat into the room?' I whispered, shutting my bedroom door behind me.

'Blood,' Donny and Red both said at once.

'Young blood,' Red added. 'That's what they like. You're the youngest, kid, so . . .'

'My blood?' I gulped.

Suddenly a pair of scissors rose out of my pencil pot and started floating through the air towards me. 'You could have warned me you were about to pick up scissors!'

'No one's picked up anything,' Red said with amusement. 'I'm using my powers of telekinesis.'

As if having invisible friends wasn't confusing enough!

The scissors floated frighteningly close to my eye. I knocked them out of the air and they clattered to the ground. 'But you know we need to lure the vampire bat with blood!' Red said sternly.

'Well, excuse me for not wanting to cut my eye open!' I said, pulling up my trouser leg. 'But I can think of a hundred better ways to make myself bleed – including picking off this scab I got when I fell off the top of the monkey ropes last week.'

I quickly picked the crusty scab off my knee and it started to bleed.

'Now open the window and sit on the window ledge so the smell of your blood catches on the wind,' said Donny. I quickly did as he said. 'Now we wait.'

So we waited . . . and waited . . . and waited . . .

I was shivering with cold and my teeth were chattering like a parrot with a point to prove. My bloody knee kept drying up and I had to keep re-picking the scab so the smell of fresh blood wafted on the wind.

It paid off.

Out of the darkness, in the dim light of the moon, I saw a bat-like shape flying silently towards me.

It perched on a branch of a nearby tree, and I could almost feel its eyes burn into me as it watched from a distance.

I got off the windowsill and inched backwards into my room.

I tried not to panic as I realized what was coming next. The vampire bat landed on my windowsill. It was within grabbing distance, but I knew the plan was to lure it right into my bedroom so we had a better chance of capturing it.

'I'm glad you came,' I said in Vampire Bat.

'The smell of your blood was so delicious, how could I have stayed away?' the bat replied with a devilish smile.

'You took my sister,' I said, trying to keep my voice as cool and calm as possible. But all I really wanted to do was scream my lungs out at the sight of the beast that kidnapped Natty. *'You've taken every child under ten in my village. You'll be coming for the older kids soon. I want you to take me first.'*

'My pleasure.' The bat's fangs glinted in the moonlight and it swooped into my room.

SLAM!

An invisible arm slammed the window shut. The vampire bat had no way out. It was trapped inside my bedroom.

The plan was now to capture it with the butterfly net and trap it in the cage that Donny had brought from the zoo.

But things did not go to plan . . .

Things went very, very wrong . . .

Before I could shout for help, before a butterfly net could swoop through the air and before anyone could come to my rescue, the vampire bat flew towards me at lightning speed.

There was no time to shout for help. I felt a sharp stab at my throat and a warm rush of blood as the bat began to drink from me.

I opened my mouth to scream but nothing came out.

My eyes clouded over and all I saw was blood.

I felt my legs go weak and the fangs in the side of my neck sank deeper and deeper into me . . .

Then all I saw was darkness.

I woke up Backstage with Mum, Dad and Grace peering over me.

'Don't try to talk, Sammy,' Mum said gently. 'You've had a little accident.'

A little accident? I was bitten by a vampire bat! This wasn't a little accident – it was as big as a bloated elephant!

'Did we . . . ?' I croaked, trying to sit up. My head was pounding and my neck throbbed like crazy. 'Did we catch it?'

'Let me out!' came an angry voice from the corner of the room.

Mum moved out of the way and I saw the vampire bat thrashing against the bars of a large cage. *'Let me out or I'll tear you all to shreds!'*

'No one here understands you except me,' I croaked at the bat, standing up shakily.

The creature stopped thrashing for a moment and looked me dead in the eye. *'Well, that's no use to me, is it? Soon you won't be able to translate anything. Can you feel it already? The lust for blood? You're becoming one of us . . . a creature of the night . . . a slave to blood . . . By this time tomorrow you'll be a vampire bat!'*

Tuesday 26th October
5 days until Halloween

When my alarm clock blasted to life this morning it felt as if something had crawled into my head and laid eggs in my skull. And it felt like those tiny eggs had hatched into maggots and were eating my brain. And the maggots were growing fatter and turning into buzzing insects that were about to fly out of my ears and nose.

In other words, MY HEAD WAS KILLING ME!!!

Sunlight streamed through the crack in my bedroom curtains and it felt as if someone was stabbing my skin with a million tiny needles. I lurched out of bed and crawled on the floor until I could reach the curtains and pull them shut – blocking out any scrap of light.

My tummy rumbled.

BLOOD!

All I wanted was blood. A nice, warm glass of thick, gloopy blood.

Yum!

No, no, not yum . . . yuk, yuk, yuk!

What is wrong with me?

All I want to do is drink blood, and stay out of the sunlight, and . . .

It's happening. Just like the vampire bat said it would.

I'm turning into one of them.

And it gets worse . . . I'm not the only one.

I somehow managed to drag myself into school today. I looked around in horror at the pale, pasty kids in my classroom. Every one of them looked as if they'd clawed their way out of a fresh grave. And every one of them had a bruise on the side of their neck, just like Natty did before she turned. Just like the one the vampire bat left me with last night.

'I don't understand,' I whispered to Mark across the classroom. 'I lured the vampire bat to me. I was the bait. That's why I was attacked. But what about you? And Tommy and Katrina and everyone else? Why have the vampire bats bitten you?'

'I don't know what you're talking about, Sammy,' Mark replied, his eyes glazed over. 'All I can think about is the blood gushing around your body. I wonder what it tastes like.'

Oh, rattlesnakes and rhino wrinkles – this is so, so bad.

'Donny!' I shouted, bursting into the Backstage offices after school. 'It's not just me who's been bitten by a vampire bat. I think they're attacking other kids at my school too.'

Donny and Red were standing next to the cage with the vampire bat in it. They both looked exhausted.

'Have you been bitten too?' I asked, alarmed.

Red shook her head. 'No, we're just tired. After you were bitten we had an urgent hissing-hinkypink report we had to check out. We were out all night fighting hissing hinkypinks in the sewers. And we've had no luck getting any information out of Vampy here.' She screwed up her face at the vampire bat.

'Why are you going after kids my age?' I asked the bat. *'Just take me — won't I be enough?'*

The vampire bat smiled its fang-tastic smile at me. *'It's time to up our game. The youngest children aren't enough any more. Soon the whole world will be like us.'*

'How can we stop that?' I asked.

'I'll never tell!' he hissed at me.

'There has to be something we can do,' I said in English, feeling hopeless. 'Is this it? Am I destined for a life of neck sucking and blood guzzling?'

GROSS!

'He's getting hungry,' Donny said thoughtfully, looking at the vampire bat. 'When he gets hungry enough, maybe then he'll talk.'

But when will that be?

How long have I got before I sprout a pair of wings and break into the nearest blood bank? Weeks? Days? Hours?

Thursday 28th October
3 days until Halloween

Five reasons why my world is worse than a weasel in a wig:

1) Half the school was off sick today. Why? They're turning into vampire bats!

2) I still haven't found a cure.

3) The hissing-hinkypink invasion is getting worse – reports are coming in every few minutes now.

4) The vampire bat we've captured still won't tell us what we need to know.

5) All I can think about is blood. Warm blood. Red blood. Gushing blood. Sweet and sticky blood. Blood. Blood. Blood!

Friday 29th October
2 days until Halloween

6 A.M.

Blood. I can't face the day outside. The thought of sunlight makes my head hurt. Blood. There's no way I can go to school, not like this. Blood.

8 A.M.

I raided the freezer — Mum always keeps a stock of raw steaks for when the moon's full and my ex-werewolf family craves blood.

Blood. Blood. Blood – I can think of nothing else. I sat on the kitchen floor and ate the raw steaks, ripping into them with my teeth like an animal. They tasted amazing.

'Sammy, what is going on?' came Mum's voice from the kitchen doorway.

Busted!

'Sammy?' she whispered again. Her voice was a horrible mix of fear and sadness. 'You too? You've been bitten too?'

I got to my feet, my legs shaking and the last scraps of raw steak in my hand. 'I'm going to find a cure, Mum, I promise.'

'No school for you today.' Mum shook her head. 'Let's get you to the zoo. I'm not always happy with Donny and Red living at the zoo – life seems so much more dangerous with them around – but if anyone has a chance of helping you, it's them.'

Mum drove me the short distance to the zoo

in her car. I covered every inch of my skin with clothes and wore a balaclava over my face – I couldn't risk a single beam of sunlight touching me. 'You'll find a cure, Sammy,' Mum said, sounding worried. 'I won't lose you. And you'll bring Natty back too, won't you? You'll find a cure. You'll find a cure.' She kept repeating the last sentence, again and again. I think she was trying to convince herself that everything was going to be OK.

I'm not going to turn into a vampire bat. I'm going to find a cure for this bloodsucking madness and bring my sister and all of the zoo animals and missing children back home.

I hope Mum's right.

I hope everything's going to be OK.

Donny and Red were nowhere to be found Backstage. They weren't in the Backstage yard or the offices. *They went out looking for hissing hinkypinks and never came back,'* came a croaking voice from behind cage bars.

It was the vampire bat.

'You must be getting really hungry by now,' I said, walking slowly towards him. *'Hungry enough to talk?'*

'Your friends have been keeping me going on tomato ketchup. It's not enough – I need blood . . . real blood.'

Blood.

Just the mention of the word had me licking my lips.

And then it struck me. Like a bolt of lightning in a storm. I'm done for. I'm never going to be 'normal' again. I've bought a one-way ticket on the vampire-bat train and I am riding it all the way to the end of the line.

'There's no cure, is there?' I whispered. My head pounded with pain and my stomach tightened into knots as I realized the truth. I was

never going to grow up to be a cryptozoologist. I was never going to travel the world in search of weird animals. I was never going to grow old and grey.

No, not me. I was going to grow fangs and hang upside down from trees.

'There is a way . . .' the vampire bat said slowly. 'You'll know what the cure is, as soon as you're one of us.'

'You're lying,' I said. 'Sphinx was one of you, and she was cured, and she has no idea how that happened.'

'The trauma of losing her colony's chief and turning back into a regular cat probably made her forget!' the bat said with a sly smile. 'But you won't forget, will you, Sammy? How could you ever forget such a thing when there's so much to lose . . . ?'

Blood rushed through my veins like a stampede of wildebeests. Could I do it? Could I turn to the dark side and come back again?

I would do anything to know what the cure was. Anything.

'*Tell me one thing . . .*' I asked. The bat nodded. '*Do you remember being human? Do you remember your name?*'

The bat shook his head. '*None of that matters now. It won't matter to you once you come with me . . . come with me . . .*' His words were hypnotic to me. All I wanted was to follow him into darkness . . .

'*OK,*' I said, licking my dry lips, '*I'm ready.*' I reached for the vampire bat's cage door. He flapped his wings in excitement and bared his fangs at me. '*You can finish me off. Turn me into one of you. If it takes me to the truth about the cure, then I'll do it. I'll find a way to come back and cure myself. You say I won't care about the cure once I'm a vampire bat. You're wrong.*'

The vampire bat smiled a wicked smile. '*Prove it.*'

I unlocked the cage and swung open the door.

The vampire bat flitted out of the cage and rose into the air, baring its jagged fangs and hissing as it spoke. *'Say goodbye to your human life, Sammy Feral!'*

No time for second thoughts.

No time to back out.

The bat swooped down, dug its claws into me and sank its fangs deep into my neck. I felt my blood pulsate and flow into its hungry bat mouth.

My eyes clouded over and I felt my life slipping further away with every beat of my heart.

'Tell me,' I managed to whisper as my legs gave way beneath me and I sank to the cold, hard floor, *'how do you cure a vampire bat?'*

The vampire bat stopped sucking and pulled its fangs from my neck. It looked me straight in the eye. *'When the chief of a colony dies, all of its bats are cured. When the chief of the Vampire Bat High Council is killed, then all of the colony chiefs die, and every vampire bat in the world will be cured. Kill Count Batula, and we all return to the creatures we once were. He's coming to the zoo on Halloween to finish you all off!'*

'How?' I screamed.

'Are you blind? Haven't you noticed the sharp rise in the hissing-hinkypink population since us bats came to town?'

Hissing hinkypinks?

He bared his fangs at me again, ready to sink them into me and take the last of my humanity. But something pulled him off me and he flew across the room as though he had been thrown.

'Sammy!' came a voice.

I looked around, desperately trying to see who was calling my name.

'Sammy!' It sounded like Donny, but he

was nowhere to be seen. 'Sammy, stay with me! Red, the cage – now!'

'On it,' came Red's voice. I couldn't see her either.

Invisible hands scooped the vampire bat up and forced him back into the cage. The lock clanked shut and the vampire bat thrashed about behind the bars. *'You tricked me!'* he hissed.

The room began to spin.

Everything was turning a bloody shade of red. Red walls. Red books on the bookshelves. Donny's pets shone in shades of scarlet, ruby and claret.

It was as though the world was drowning in blood.

'Sammy!' came Donny's voice again. 'We're here – we're covered in panda snot. We saw the whole thing. What did he say to you? Did he tell you the cure?'

'Donny,' I muttered, as my eyelids grew

heavy, 'I think it's too late for me. I think it's all over. You need to kill Count Batula – he's coming here on Halloween. If you kill him, then every vampire bat in the world will be cured. Hissing hinkypinks – somehow they . . . Donny!' I gasped. 'Help me! I can feel my life slipping away. It's too late! I think I'm turning into . . . into . . . into . . .'

Saturday 30th October
1 day until Halloween

I am one fang-tacular toothache away from becoming a vampire bat.

But I'm not there yet.

You can't kill Sammy Feral that easily!

But my limbs are growing stiff, and my skin is as pale as chalk. Just the thought of sunlight makes my skin burn, and my need for blood is getting impossible to ignore.

I can feel the vampire virus running through my veins and beginning to change me. I'm feeling less human by the minute. It would feel more natural to flap my arms about and fly through the sky than to hold a pen and write.

I don't know how long I've got left. But one thing I do know for certain . . . if Count Batula doesn't die soon, then I'll be sinking my teeth into the nearest neck by sunset tomorrow.

I've spent today Backstage, drifting in and out of consciousness. Donny and Red have been feeding me raw steaks from the lion-feed fridges whenever I'm awake.

Even though I've been asleep, I'm aware of people coming to visit me. Mum sat by my bed and sobbed, begging me to get better. Dad came and ruffled my hair and told me to pull through. Grace was here – I think she was holding my hand but I'm not sure; I may have been dreaming. And at one point I woke up and saw Sphinx sitting at the foot of my bed, having a conversation with the wish frog about what they should do if I turn into a vampire bat. I can't remember exactly what they said, but I know they're worried.

I'm worried.

I don't know if I'll ever be OK again.

Some time this evening Donny and Red came and sat by my bed. 'Sammy, wake up. We've got a plan that we think might work.'

'It involves hissing hinkypinks and you, Sammy,' Red said, her black lipstick curling into a smile.

'What do you need me to do?' I croaked, trying to sit up in bed.

Donny and Red glanced at each other, took a deep breath and then looked at me.

'It's simple,' Donny said. 'Just bare your neck, and let the vampire bats bite . . .'

Sunday 31st October
Halloween

2 P.M.

The Backstage offices are overflowing with spray cans of disinfectant. Donny and Red have stocked up ahead of the Zoo of the Year award ceremony tonight.

'We'll need them to fight off the hissing hinkypinks,' Red told Sphinx when she asked about them.

'And how are hissing hinkypinks going to defeat Count Batula?' Sphinx asked, swishing her tail.

'What's the one thing that vampire bats

are scared of?' Red asked.

'Sunlight,' Sphinx replied without thinking.

'And what do we know about hissing hinkypink sick?' Red prompted.

'It emits UV rays . . .' Sphinx said thoughtfully. 'So you're planning to . . .'

'Everyone knows that the mere sight of a child makes a hissing hinkypink vomit radioactive sludge,' Donny explained. 'We need to lure the hissing hinkypinks into the zoo during the ceremony tonight. We know that Count Batula is planning to attack the zoo, so they're our only chance of defeating him. Once Count Batula is here, then all we need to do is get the hissing hinkypinks to vomit at the sight of Sammy. The vomit emits strong UV light — it's a long shot, but it's all we've got.'

'Just the thought of sunlight makes my skin burn,' I croaked from my deathbed in the corner of the room.

'Exactly.' Red smirked. 'So the UV light from the hissing hinkypink's upchuck should be enough to kill a weird vampire bat – even one as powerful as Count Batula.'

'I can't believe we didn't think of this sooner.' Donny shook his head of grey hair. 'The rise in hissing-hinkypink sightings and the vampire bats coming to town was more than just a coincidence. Every venom has an antidote . . .'

'We need to be careful that we only kill Count Batula,' Sphinx said, sounding worried. 'We don't want to kill the other bats – we want to cure them.'

'Don't worry,' Donny reassured her. 'We have a plan.'

9 P.M.

Things needed for our plan to defeat Count Batula:

* Decomposing toilet paper (to lure hissing hinkypinks to the zoo)
* Children (to make the hissing hinkypinks vomit)
* Count Batula bait (so we can separate him from the other vampire bats)

I spent the day in bed dreaming about blood and flying through the night sky as a vampire bat. The dreams were getting more and more realistic, and I knew that it wouldn't be long before the transformation was complete.

I was so sick I couldn't help Donny and Red hide decomposing toilet paper around the zoo to lure the hissing hinkypinks. They roped in Grace and Max to help.

'But what about the Zoo of the Year committee?' I heard Dad say. 'They'll be arriving tonight – how are we going to explain the stench of rotten toilet paper?'

'And how are we going to explain that there aren't any animals?' Mum pointed out. 'At least if we do what Donny asks us to, we have a hope of getting the zoo animals back. And, honestly, who cares about the Zoo of the Year award? All I care about is getting Natty back, and making sure Sammy is well again. I'd do anything to have my children safe, including littering the zoo with decomposing loo roll!'

By the time the sun set and the Zoo of the Year committee arrived, Feral Zoo stank worse than a sewage plant on a sunny day.

'Whatever is that ghastly smell?' complained the chief judge, holding his nose in disgust. 'And where are all the animals?' he asked,

looking around at the empty animal enclosures.

'As you know,' Dad told the committee, 'we've had an unfortunate outbreak of deadly bat flu at the zoo over the last week. The animals are still recovering away from the public eye, although we hope that they will be making an appearance later.'

'And the smell?' one woman asked, choking on the poo-filled fumes.

'Drains,' Mum smiled, offering no further explanation.

The sun had set and a small sliver of moon was rising higher in the night sky. Dad had erected a small stage by the lions' den, which was where the Zoo of the Year award presentation was taking place. As soon as it was dark enough, Donny and Red helped me out of the Backstage yard and into the main zoo.

The smell of humans wafted on the breeze, making me lick my lips with thirst. My hearing was getting more bat-like, and I could hear the blood pulsating through everyone's veins . . . All I wanted to do was sink my teeth into people and drink!

'Remember the plan, Sammy,' Donny whispered in my ear as he led me towards the lions' den. 'Once the bats arrive, then you make a play for Count Batula and lead him . . .'

'We are here today,' boomed the chief judge's voice from the stage, 'to celebrate Feral Zoo winning Zoo of the Year for the fourth time.'

I blinked and looked around. Dozens of people were sitting in seats, looking up at the small stage by the empty lions' den. Mum, Dad, Grace and Max, the Zoo of the Year committee and a bunch of other official-looking people and newspaper reporters were all staring up at the chief inspector as he gave a speech about excellence in zoo-keeping and high standards of rare animal breeding. I found it difficult to concentrate on what he was saying – all I could focus on was the pain in my throat. It felt dryer than a camel in a desert. I needed blood . . .

My teeth began to itch. Something sharp prodded my bottom lip, and I reached my hand to my mouth – I had grown fangs! My breathing quickened . . . this was it . . . I was beginning to transform into a bat!

I looked up into the night sky as I felt my human life slipping away from me.

That's when I heard them . . . The flapping of thousands of wings flying towards us through the darkness. Exhilaration ran through me – the thought of the vampire bats didn't fill me with dread, like it was supposed to. Instead it made me excited. I wanted to join them. I wanted to rise up into the sky and fly away with them. I was ready to become one of them.

One by one the guests lifted their heads to the sky and watched as a plague of bats descended on

Feral Zoo. There were thousands of them. Their eyes glowed in the darkness and their dagger fangs glinted like diamonds. Everywhere you looked there were bats – perched on the fence, hanging from tree branches, sitting on the lawn and swarming like locusts in the air above us.

To normal people, the sight would make your skin crawl.

But not to me. Not in my semi-vampire state. To me the sight was beautiful.

I looked up into the sky and watched as a giant vampire bat swooped down. The biggest one of all. Count Batula. He hovered above the stage, his hungry eyes glaring at the crowd. *'Attack!'* he shouted.

At his command the bats rose up into the air before diving into the crowd. Baring their teeth, they chomped down on the nearest necks they could find.

'Help!'

'No!

'Save us!' people screamed around me.

Members of the crowd got to their feet and flapped their arms in the air, trying desperately to fight off the bats. But it was no use – the humans were outnumbered a thousand to one. No one was getting out of this alive.

I looked on as Mum and Dad were swallowed by the swarm of bats. I heard them call out my name as the bats attacked them. 'Sammy!' Mum screamed. 'Remember the plan!'

The plan?

With every breath I took I was becoming more bat-like. Plan? What plan? . . . What was I meant to do?

A vampire bat soared through the air towards me. He bared his fangs, ready to bite. *'Not Sammy Feral!'* came Count Batula's voice from among the crowd. *'He's mine!'*

The plan . . . I could just about remember what I had to do.

I tried to focus with every scrap of strength I had. I ignored the urge to join the bats and guzzle blood.

My heavy legs carried me forward. Through the swarm of bats I could see two beady eyes watching me. It was him, Count Batula. All I had to do was lead him away from the lions' den and towards the drain cover by the tiger enclosure . . .

I plodded forward, trying to focus. 'Don't

think about blood, don't think about blood,' I repeated to myself.

Blood. Blood. Blood.

My feet dragged along the ground as I made my way towards the tiger enclosure, just like we'd planned.

I was nearly there. I could see Donny and Red by the drain cover, ready to lift it and unleash the hissing hinkypinks into the zoo. Suddenly my legs gave way beneath me and I fell to the ground with a thud. I tried to crawl forward, towards the drain.

I felt my fingers pull apart and skin stretch between them.

Arrrggghhh!!!

The pain was excruciating! I looked to my sides, to where my arms and hands should have been, but my arms had disappeared. In their place I had sprouted wings. Bat wings.

Giant, furry, skin-like bat wings.

Great galloping gazelles! It was too late for me now!

I looked down, and where my legs used to be were two spindly bird-like legs.

I was almost a bat!

There was no way I was going to make it to the drain cover. I couldn't lead Count Batula to the hissing hinkypinks, so I'd have to lead them to him.

I saw a stray piece of rotten toilet paper caught in a nearby tree branch. It would have to do.

My humanity was slipping away. I couldn't remember my name or who my family were or why I was there at the zoo. All I could think about was blood, and needing to drink it.

'*Sammy Feral,*' said Count Batula. He was hovering above me, his eyes glowing red. '*You are becoming one of us. Don't be scared. Embrace your death, and the new life that awaits you.*'

I felt my eyes shrink into bird-like beads, and my ears grow big and hairy as I transformed into a weird vampire bat.

'*Come to me,*' I managed to say to Count Batula, as I drew my last human breath. '*Closer.*'

Count Batula hovered nearer to me. He was now so close to the piece of toilet paper in the tree.

'Now!' I heard Donny shout.

With my supersensitive bat hearing I heard the sound of a heavy drain cover being dragged along the ground. Then the air filled with the screeching of hundreds of hissing hinkypinks. I looked behind me. The pink rat-like creatures were crawling out of the drain — their bodies shimmering in the moonlight. They squealed in delight like frenzied pigs as they began to gobble up the toilet paper that we had littered around the zoo.

They came towards me, just as we'd hoped they would . . . but none of them were puking. I looked too bat-like — the plan would never work!

I had failed.

I felt my heart stop inside my chest and I exhaled my last human breath. My wings flapped into the air and I rose. It was over. I had died and turned into a vampire bat. Count Batula hadn't been defeated, and Natty, the missing children and the zoo animals would never be saved.

But I didn't care.

All I cared about was my thirst for blood.

I looked down, ready to dig my claws into the flesh of the nearest human and feed. That's when I spotted a boy – Mark.

'Over here!' Mark shouted, waving his arms towards the hissing hinkypinks.

As the hissing hinkypinks turned to look at Mark, I felt a butterfly net sweep through the air and snatch me out of the sky. The net pulled me to the ground and a blanket was thrown over me, shielding me from what was about to happen . . .

From beneath the blanket I heard the sound of the hissing hinkypinks vomiting at the sight of Mark.

'*What's happening to me?*' I heard Count Batula scream.

'It's working!' Donny shouted.

With my new bat eyes I could see the UV glare, and it felt as though I had flown into the centre of the sun. I heard Count Batula screaming and the hissing hinkypinks scurrying back into the sewer in fear.

I felt my wings begin to shrivel and my ears shrank back down to human size.

Then the world went black.

Monday 1st November

Mark was sitting on the end of my bed when I woke up. 'When Donny and Red realized that you would never make it, they called me and asked for my help,' he said proudly. 'I knew it was risky, but what choice did I have?'

'If you hadn't stepped in and made the hissing hinkypinks vomit at the sight of you then we'd all have been doomed,' Donny said.

Everyone was gathered around my little camp bed in the Backstage offices. Dad was drinking tea, Natty was cuddled up in Mum's lap and Grace was kneeling on the floor beside me. 'I suppose you're used to things vomiting at the sight of you,' Grace joked to Mark.

'I can't believe I didn't see Count Batula burst into flames.' I shook my head. 'I always miss out on all the cool stuff.'

'You realize you would have burst into flames too,' Red raised her eyebrows. 'You were a vampire bat at that point. I saved your life by trapping you in that butterfly net and shielding you from the UV rays.'

'So let me get this straight.' I sat upright in bed. 'As soon as Count Batula burst into flames then all the other vampire bats turned back into their normal selves?'

Red nodded. 'Including you, Sammy,'

'And me.' Natty smiled.

'And Matthew,' said Sphinx. 'Remember, we met his mother in Barren Heath? She asked me to thank you for bringing her son home to her.'

'Towards the end I think we were all close

to becoming vampire bats,' Dad admitted. 'Thank you, Donny and Red, for once again getting us all out of a bit of a pickle.'

'And what about the Zoo of the Year award?' I asked.

'Anyone who was bitten last night,' said Donny, 'which was basically the entire Zoo of the Year committee, can't remember a thing about what happened.'

'And the zoo animals?' I asked.

'All back in their enclosures, and back to their old selves,' Mum said with a smile. 'Well, back to their old selves with one slight change . . .'

'What?' I asked.

'They can speak human languages,' Sphinx informed me. 'Just like I can. You know, you and I are not so different now, Sammy. Both reformed vampire bats. Both committed to a life protecting the world from evil creatures. Thank you, Sammy.'

'For what?' I asked.

'For helping and not judging me for what I once was,' she replied.

'No worries.' I smiled.

Wow. That was definitely one weird weekend . . . a healthy 9.5 on the Feral Scale of Weirdness.

Not only did I die and become a vampire bat, but I was a key part of a plan that killed the evil Count Batula and cured every vampire bat in existence. And now I can talk to every animal in the zoo if I want to, not just the weird ones.

Life rocks!

Monday 8th November

There is finally a happy ending to the terrible tale of missing children. Hundreds of children who had gone missing from their homes have been returned to their families.

Girls and boys rushed into the arms of their parents, but none of them can remember where they have been or how they came to be saved.

'I don't remember anything,' said Matthew, aged 12, who vanished from the village of Barren Heath several weeks ago. 'All I remember is dreaming that I had wings and could fly. I'm so happy that I'm home.'

It would appear that the children have all . . .

Story continues on page 7

It's been a whole week since I was cured of being a vampire bat. Not many people grow fangs and sprout wings and live to tell the tale. I don't even crave blood any more. How cool is that? Am I weird for thinking that my life is awesome?!

Sphinx has decided to stick around Backstage at the zoo for a while. Maybe the wish frog is right – maybe you can never trust a talking cat. But if that's true then we can't trust the lions, elephants, anteaters or flying squirrels either – every one of them could speak to us if they wanted to.

Mum made me and Natty go back to school the very next day after we were cured. It's so unfair – most people's parents would let them miss at least a week of school if they became a vampire bat!

But, oh no, not my mum.

'Absolutely not, Sammy.' She shook her

head. 'If I let you miss school every time you turned into a vampire bat or were kissed by a yeti or cursed by a Hell Hound, then you'd get no education at all!'

Maybe she had a point.

'But I can have my lessons at the zoo,' I argued. 'I can have cryptozoology lessons. Donny can teach me about hissing hinkypinks and gremlins and mothmen. Just last week we had a report in of talking garden gnomes. If I'm at normal school then I don't get to learn about that kind of stuff, which is way more important.'

'Evenings and weekends,' Mum said firmly. 'That's when you'll have your lessons with Donny, and only if you've done your zoo chores!'

I suppose that's fair enough. Someone has to sweep out the sea lions and groom the gorillas.

I'm on my way to the zoo now. As soon as I've cleaned out the bird-eating-spider tanks

I'm heading Backstage to catch up with the crypto-gang. I had a text from Donny earlier saying there was something he needed my help investigating . . . I wonder what it could be?

Wriggling river sprites? Sneaky snotlings? Bouncing boggarts? Mud-gobbling hobgoblins?

Who knows what's in store for me next. But I can't wait to find out!

Sammy ☺

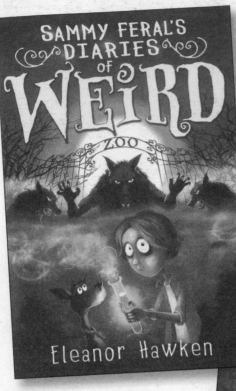

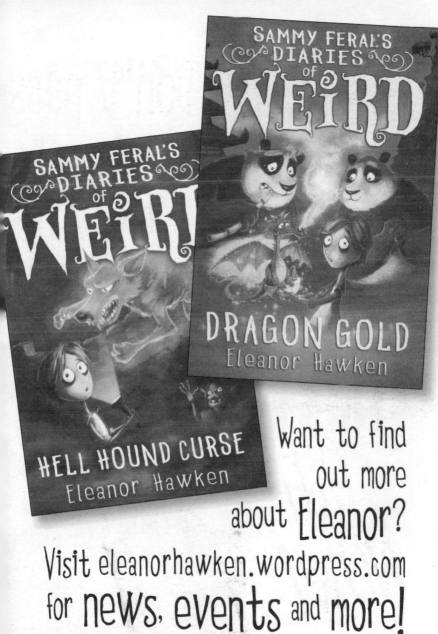

Don't miss
Eleanor Hawken's amazing new series

FELIX FROST
TIME DETECTIVE

Coming soon!

www.quercusbooks.co.uk

Quercus